ACKNOWLEDGMENTS

There are many people whose support has contributed to the American edition of my book.

Amelia Antonucci, the Director of the Italian Cultural Institute of San Francisco; Rochelle Pichetti and Gloria Gerolami, who still believe in talent; Alice Goldberg and the Association "Il filo d'Oro." All sustained me with their kindness and generosity.

In particular I thank Margie Waller for her friendship and patient encouragement during my adventurous journey into the mysteries of the English language.

But it is most of all to the extraordinary care and attention of City Lights editor Nancy J. Peters that I owe this *Medusa*.

MEDUSA

TRANSLATOR'S PREFACE

The fabled waters of the Mediterranean Sea unite lands where ancient myths still permeate experience in a sleepy sort of way. The stories that lie at the heart of European and European-American cultures are more tangible in Italy than in California. The Mediterranean, moreover, is the center of an Africa-Europe nexus every bit as much as it is a focal point of European history. It is also the common sea of Europe and the Near East. Its ancient gods, goddesses and mythological figures stand as testimony to a time when cultures now too vastly differentiated in American notions of the world shared one of the earth's major pulse points.

Whenever a contemporary Italian writer awakens one of the Mediterranean's slumbering myths, we understand that it had never died. Thus the myth of Medusa, who many of us see only as a horrid, severed, snake-covered head, the very vision of female menace, comes to us anew in Marina Minghelli's intriguing, hermetic first novel. Here, Minghelli treats us to a privileged view of Medusa the girl, a pensive, bewildered beauty whose quest is complicated by her need to understand the complex reactions she causes in others. Through this charming, doomed personage and her counterpart in the novel's contemporary plot, we are given an inside look at the challenges and promise of the feminine today.

Marina Minghelli offers a new, very new, reading of the Medusa myth, intertwined with components of esoteric traditions and the sometimes harsh realities of love and desire in modern-day Rome. In this, she follows in the footsteps of Pier Paolo Pasolini, whose own radical reworkings of Mediterranean myths defined and critiqued the politics of Italy in the sixties. In *Medusa*, Minghelli makes imaginative use of psychoanalysis, literary theory, and ancient traditions to create for her complex contemporary protagonist a journey of transformation toward empowerment and independence.

Beverly Allen

To my mother,
and to everyone like her

Three things are too wonderful for me,
four I do not understand:
the way of an eagle in the sky,
the way of a snake on the rock,
the way of a ship on the high seas,
and a way of a man with a girl.

Proverbs. 30, 18–19

SKETCH OF AN IMAGE TO GIVE AS A GIFT

"I never ask for what I cannot give"
—*after* M. *Sosa*

A STUDY FOR A Story
A Script
Something else

First Subject
Meeting between a man and a woman. He is 40 years old, she, 33. There are two meeting places: the piazza and his house. The story is reconstructed and seen through her eyes.

Second Subject
Medusa

PREAMBLE

Reconstructing a love story and detaching it from a woman's life like a slice from a cake has forced me to mark clear borders and cut decisively.

A go at it.

A love story, moreover, swollen like a cistern in spring-time. To set my hand to it was to live like someone who, too long silent, feels any chance of emitting sound disappear.

The danger of water is very different from that of fire, dear to men departing on journeys.

And this is certainly no time for a wedding.

PROLOGUE

The piazza, July 30, 1984

She was sitting at the dark front door on uneven, age-softened steps. Leaning back, she watched what was going on. It was evening, late. Rome more beautiful than ever and the piazza a magic circle, a breath of sounds, all of them, captured and then presented like a gift. As soon as she got home she felt the pleasure of her place.

She and her girlfriend, who now sits beside her like a waiting puppy, had come in during the afternoon. Once home, an agitated feeling—though she tried to deny it—had forced her out to walk through the habitual streets. Few words to her foreign girlfriend, who wanted to know everything. Before taking her along, she'd cut her off, "You have to discover the magic of this city yourself, and perhaps it's best to do it without talking." Relaxing now at last on the still-warm stone, she rests her eyes on the girl. "Maritza, God isn't holding back anything tonight." She laughs. "I have no memories, I know nothing, and tonight memory isn't eating up my life." She has a comic look, a little girl with wrinkles. Slowly she begins to roll a cigarette. Her face drawn in concentration, she begins to speak again. "I like being here. This piazza is like a track into my different lives." Laughter. "The great past . . . we even put on a play over there between the two fountains." The cigarette has come apart, she licks it slowly. "But for some time now, coming back here does something else to me. I want to run into a man I met a year ago."

Excited now, Maritza asks her to tell the story. "So,

during a seminar I'd met some young women who used to hang out at places near here. It was spring and I wanted to be out and about again. Another world. It wasn't my crowd, and anyway my crowd didn't exist any more." Her gaze embraces the whole piazza. "I wanted to play." A mischievous smile. "I wanted to forget myself. It was still my country-house phase. I was living in halves, city and country, the last stop before the end. I had met Alessandro at a party. Best not to talk about the party. For a time I watched and, Maritza, I wondered about the women. Ten years erased. As if that were possible. Worse, much worse. These retro parties—how to put it. They mark people's faces with a new dreariness. Anyway, the women defeated. It's hard to learn to laugh about this, too." Her own face changes constantly. Maritza reflects it like a mirror.

"Alessandro was watching too. He was sitting next to me. A little earlier I had seen him sitting across the room. He was handsome, but I still didn't like him. I don't know how to say it, it was the kind of handsome that dries its hair with a hair dryer." Maritza laughs out loud. She continues. "He spoke to me, questions mostly, smart ones, smart observations. He'd surprised me. But I was distracted, watching the way Gianni moved. I'd decided I liked Gianni and once I'd chosen my object of desire, everything went in that direction, as usual.

"Later we ended up at Alessandro's house.

"I remember the trip back and how, as soon as we got here behind the piazza, he climbed out of one of the cars and invited us all in.

"The house in the alley. The alleys of Rome make me feel like I'm in a labyrinth already explored. We walked up to a dark, shabby door. Steep stairs to the tiny landing, and a bike leaning against the banister.

"Then I went in. You should have seen that house. A kind of past collected and compressed into two shadowy rooms, alive but already completed. A different memory that nonetheless reminds you of your own. The front door opens directly onto the first room. The walls completely submerged in books, records, and paintings. Hard to find a place to sit. Two easy chairs, as if they were just passing through, an old buffet and small tables laden with objects. In a corner a ladder holding all the stereo parts and, just in front of the door, a window set back and completely hidden behind old lace curtains.

"I stayed there by the books, fascinated. He came in right away, talking, and took me into the other room. Here, too, everything full, books and more books and a huge bed reflected in a mirrored wall, maybe that's why it seemed so big. On one side a low dresser made a pathway leading to the bathroom, on the other side was a minuscule kitchen.

"It's more a den, I'd say, the lights are low and only in the corners.

"I saw it only once but it's as if it has grown inside me." She falls silent, her face drawn and distant.

Maritza asks her to go on. She gazes at the piazza and at Maritza waiting there, smiles and takes her hand. "I'd really like you to see the scene. He talks, asks me questions, shows me things. He's very attentive, he wants to discover what I'm like the way I myself would. But with that bed right there, I didn't feel comfortable, I was almost afraid, strangely enough, not relaxed. There was something that didn't convince me, and deep down I didn't recognize him. Even his dog, such a huge dog in such a little house, was out of place, he couldn't even move around. I wondered why that dog.

"He was half lying down on the bed, and he asked me to

sit down with the most offhand gesture (the dog was on the bed, too) and the whole time he was reading an article, a study of the origins of the sun myth. Nice, but his voice was put on, he was reciting, his 'r' was accentuated still more. All my fine rules went crazy. I listened, I watched, fascinated and amused at the same time.

"It's incredible how all this is engraved in my memory. I don't know when and why, but in time his image began to come to me more and more often. I started to remember, to relive, to see other things.

"That evening, though, I went back to the others as soon as I could. I wanted to be with Gianni, so I left. I said goodbye. He was sitting on the chair by the window. I bent down and gave him a kiss. He asked why I was leaving, if I didn't like it there. His beautiful clear blue eyes were so serious, and he said, 'I haven't figured out why you're taking off, but I'll find out.' I smiled without answering, almost embarrassed. It wasn't hard to find out, I left with Gianni.

"A weird time. The next day I was at my still unfinished house in Rome. At that point one of the girls I had gone out with was staying there and Tiziana was always around too. On the first afternoon, Gianni and I were still in the bedroom, I hear people come in and among their voices, unmistakable, is Alessandro's. Argument with Gianni and decision not to go out (but I would have liked to). Alessandro's voice had reached me loud and clear, a challenge. Talking nonsense was his thing. I liked his paradoxes and the ridiculous way people answered. A favorite phrase came to mind, 'If you know it I'll tell you, if you don't, I won't.'

"And yet I liked his intelligence at a distance. And his pain I understood later, during the winter. Maybe I began to resemble him. I don't know. I saw him again a couple of times in the bar, briefly, scarcely a hello. But Tiziana hung out with him and told me about him. Alessandro did nothing but ask what was happening between me and Gianni. I felt gratified.

"It seems he's with someone who's very young, but no one knows anything more. His story, his work. As if he were living a total mystery. All of that disappeared almost immediately. But he's still around."

She stretches. "And I thought I had no memories tonight!" Her sharp voice startles Maritza, her attention lost who knows where.

She lights a cigarette and loses herself again in the passing scene.

Then suddenly the piazza returns, its sounds and colors, like crickets when they all start to sing at once.

Not much time had passed when she sees him. He was hanging around looking distracted, like someone who doesn't have anything to do, there by the paintings, right in front of them.

She takes Maritza's arm slowly and squeezes it. "It's him." And Maritza, "Where, call him." The girl's eyes are shining almost as much as her own. And she, softly, "If he turns around I'll call him, only if he turns around."

He sees her. She raises her arm and a smile.

He comes over, his lips set, and his voice, "Well, look who's here! My old friend!" He is handsome, tan. She smiles, amused at what she's thinking. She shoos away the image of a sun lamp. She looks right into his eyes, an instant out of time. "Vision" has always marked her life. A prisoner of the image, she regularly chose to let it live. She had never figured out why, knowing what it cost.

She greets him. She lets herself be taken over by this chance meeting.

Power seizes her and raises her like the rising wind.

They look at each other. They have the same smile, the moment has come.

He sits down next to her, a thread connects them at once, their legs touch. The war of words begins. Maritza looks on, fascinated.

He – "Where have you put your boyfriend, tell me." She is puzzled for a minute, then laughs. He goes on, "I hear he left you pretty fast." She laughs and hinting at an imitation of his irony answers, "Hmm, I didn't know you'd been hearing about me . . . ."

She seems pierced by her smile, like a spiral of light in the dark or a lantern shining far away. She is determined, disarming. She doesn't relinquish his eyes, and the heat of his leg can't lie. While he manages a conversation pieced together out of trivia and incitements, she thinks, "I want you tonight."

First Day

His house. July 30, 1984

They're still talking on the stairs. He seems more accessible. The sneer shaped by his unlit cigarette forgotten. His attentive voice accompanies the desire in his eyes. Conquest, never complete, is nonetheless sufficient if she acknowledges him. Books the intermediary. The proof in every connection. They scrutinize each other for a moment and start up again. She, ever more emotional. He, intrigued.

The game continues. At his house he can give her the titles of the books that interest her.

The three of them go off in silence. But, as if he couldn't resist for long, Alessandro teases Maritza every now and then, pressing her with questions that don't need responses.

She seems absent. She walks slightly apart from the others and attends to her own thoughts, troubled. She is like an animal when it suddenly raises its nose and sniffs the air. She begins to perspire. She notices his stronger odor. Her mouth is warm and her lips are dry. She knows what that means.

Steps in the dark alley. The door, the stairs, she doesn't remember them being so steep, and finally his house.

They go in. Maritza is at the stereo right away. Alessandro walks around self-assured. She remains silent, looking around. She wants a cigarette but her hands are trembling, she's not able to roll it. Now and then their eyes meet, both of them serious. She begins to wonder how it will happen.

She doesn't want to worry about it. Bewildered, she sees her early happiness fly away. Her silence grows.

The three of them are half lying on the bed, obviously the heart of the house. The dog has been sent to the other room, a difference, she thinks. The dog has sad eyes, he's all done in.

Now Alessandro has stretched out next to her. The mirrors offer more beautiful images, maybe it's the low lights in the corners.

The exasperated voice, the one that always seemed to need to cause destruction, is somehow appeased. The conversation he leads now is slower. Chat about music with Maritza, who is happy to have found records from her country. And almost absentmindedly he begins to touch her lightly.

Tense at first, she pretends not to notice. Later, she no longer tries to hide her quick breathing, at moments she closes her eyes, already drowned, the better to feel his hand that grazes her hair, her forehead, her shoulders.

Maritza goes to put on a record and stays in the other room. Alessandro, who had gone with her, comes back. They look at each other, he speaks as he comes toward her, his face a few inches from hers, he kisses her. A strange, tight kiss. His face leaning forward, completely transformed, he doesn't come in. Even his lips press closed like an offering never made. She seeks his closed eyes, doesn't find them. Her lips, lost, tremble violently and she can't stop them. She is disconcerted. She feels his body in a way she hasn't felt for much too long, an almost intolerable presence, a sound too loud. He presses her to him as if he would never again let her leave.

All kinds of messages clash inside her, that body that flows over her like precious liquid and that hand, tenacious, that immediately touches her cunt.

She – "Stop. I don't want to make love like this." Eyes closed, he smiles vaguely, "You're right." But he keeps on.

The whole thing lasts twenty minutes, one side of a record. He – "The music is about to end. What do I do?"

She doesn't answer. "Please, don't go." But she doesn't say it aloud. He is inside her, repeats his question.

She – "I don't know. . . go." And she thinks it's like that time she tore off her own adhesive bandages. He gets up, straightens himself out. Lying still, she watches him. The record is over, he'd gauged the time well.

He, his back to her, before he goes away, "My head's spinning." She laughs softly, her hands over her eyes.

Maritza comes in just then, looks at her perplexed. She slowly straightens her clothes. They smile, accomplices.

He returns. Again, the three there on the bed. She, more silently than before, thinks, "This is how you do it, this is the control you're looking for. You ought to take some lessons. I don't want to think." Lying there with her eyes closed, she feels his hand touching her again, his hot body behind her. "So it's not over yet." She listens to him tell about journeys, countries, wondrous things.

She fantasizes about him, a man who's traveled the world.

All of a sudden he asks her softly, "Are you staying here tonight?"

She – "I don't know, there's Maritza, I have to ask her."

He – "You could both stay, it's a big bed."

She doesn't know. Maritza doesn't want to go home alone, and she wants to stay.

Finally he decides. He makes the bed, takes a pillow and winks at the girl, "Don't worry, dear, I'll be like a brother to you!" They get undressed. In only his tee-shirt, he walks through the house, relaxed. He turns out the light and comes back to bed. As soon as he's there, in the middle, he turns toward her.

They start to make love.

Their bodies join right away. She loves him fearlessly, ardent and grateful that she still can. She accepts that true body that doesn't know how to play a role very well, that head locked in and vigilant like an insomniac dragon in front of its cave.

She laughs, allows herself words long forbidden: it's beautiful, I feel you, love.

He says nothing. Brief pauses, her laughter dies by itself, but she seems not to notice.

She – "Sorry, I'm a little silly." It's like a confession, whispered.

He – "I don't know what you are, I only know that you're not silly." His casual voice is a little hoarse.

She, happy, caresses him. She knows to touch him behind and she does it, he takes her that way, too. She feels pain and gently tells him so, "If it's not too important for you." And he, "I thought you liked it." A breath caught in his throat and then, softly, "I don't know what matters to me."

They touch each other slowly. She, inside the echo of that last phrase, finds the proof.

With the voice of someone nearing with caution, he asks, "What do you think? Is your friend asleep?"

She, calmly, "I don't think so."

He – "Neither do I." Perplexed, he continues, "How does this situation strike you? It's a little unusual, don't you think?"

She smiles in the dark but wants to laugh crazily.

Feeling suddenly liberated, she thinks, "So this is what an emperor is like at rest without his armor when no one's watching. Seers must have felt like this when they had just finished a difficult omen."

To him, "I'm fine and to tell the truth, I hadn't even thought about it."

She begins caressing and touches him again. She hears a cry screamed out in silence.

She feels him arrive completely. He rises up, frantically searching. Stretched above her, his nervous fingers rifle behind the bed. She doesn't get it. Then he puts something in her hand. Yes, now she understands and finally hears an unrecognizable voice that begs, "Take me, take me." Then she stops, he turns over on his back, still. She looks at him in the dark and asks, "What's wrong?" Cold, he answers, "Nothing."

She remains silent. For an instant, she gazes at a little red light high up on the wall and then decides not to hear the still distant sound. She frantically blocks the silence that invades her. She wants to return to the path she was on before, go all the way and live that possibility, the final door. Stretched out next to him, she slowly moves her hand, seeks the still fresh traces. She comes to his eyes, touches them, and then one shoulder, the other. Now she is on top and inside him.

He comes first and brusquely pulls himself away. "I told you to stop, you take too many chances, I don't want to leave anything lying around." He gets up suddenly and goes to wash. She is infinitely tired, she doesn't want to move, to get dressed. That red point also gives off a light hiss, she hadn't noticed it before, it catches her eye. Lucid, she admits that the bells had rung, she hadn't wanted to hear them. She feels like someone who contemplates. She looks at her hands lying on her body as if they'd been cut off.

He returns, lies down next to her in perfect control of himself. Right away he starts to speak in an inexhaustible and polished manner as if, now rested, he had been able to tap unexpected reserves. "Here," she tells herself, "the emperor has returned in fancy dress." Everything is as it had been at the start. The sentence of repetition begins.

He talks about when they had met a year earlier, makes fun of her and her affair with Gianni. She lets him talk, prefers to listen to the memories that, awakened by his words, make her smile.

She – "But you were very curious."

He – "I'm always curious, about everyone, I like to watch people."

She – "And it doesn't bother you not to be a part of things?"

He – "I'm not always on the outside. Only as much as you need to be to take care of yourself and get what you want. I grew up on the streets, I understood right away. If I wanted what others had, I needed money. I got it, I met people, learned about the world and how to get along in it. Now it's time to let all that experience pay off." He watches her in the dark, his voice ironic, "Maybe you can't understand, you're too simple, and at one with yourself."

She thinks that's the most beautiful thing she's ever heard. "Life's funny, it's as if he's just told me I'm a piece of shit." And to him, "But do you ever get involved?" "Yes, of course, but it never lasts long." It seems like a warning. She goes on, "And what do you do to make a living?" "Whatever comes along. Steal, deal, it doesn't matter." The words streak across her like whistling bullets. She listens to that discordant, distorted voice. She'd like to shut him up, hold him, feel once again the heat of his so true and real body. She can't, tired as she is of following hidden signals.

His edgy voice continues strong and sure, it recognizes her defeat. Every so often meanings she has disavowed adhere to her. Power, dominion, supremacy. The words win. The wind on the hill has torn the kites. He is far away. Closed and distant, he turns his back on her. As soon as she has answered good-night, she begins once again to stare at the little red light, immerses herself in her thoughts. "This is reality, my dear. I'm so tired, it's almost morning. One night of love, so to speak, even here I'm alone."

She moves ever so slightly, searches for his legs, without his noticing she brushes against them, smiles. She remembers the times it was she who turned her back. "Everything means something whether you like it or not." The images file past. She listens to their breathing. Maritza is sleeping, Alessandro, too. The light filters in, it's dawn. She hears the ancient sound of the day being born, she, always the last one to fall asleep. Her eyes grow calm. Cuddled up closer to him, her last thought passes over her like a falling star, "Funny, there's always one bird that manages to sing."

At nine in the morning he gets up, makes coffee, dresses, remembers to give her a kiss.

He's in a hurry. He – "I'll buy you breakfast at Giolitti's." "If you hurry up," she thinks. She wakes Maritza, they dress quickly and off they go. The sun is shining brightly there where the alleys meet.

Maritza goes ahead with her bicycle, the two of them arm in arm a ways behind and the dog, happy at last.

Neither one speaks. Outside the café brief embarrassment and then he in a distracted way, "Where are you two going?"

She – "We're going to walk around here in the center of town."

He – "Great, I'll say good-bye, the dog can't be out without a leash."

He looks at her, "Will you give me your phone number?"

She – "Yes, have you got a pen?"

He – "I don't need one, I'll memorize it."

Quickly, her smile recites the numbers. He brusquely

offers her his cheek. His mouth is busy with his unlit cigarette.

They say goodbye almost without stopping and their eyes do not meet.

EXCERPTS FROM HER WRITINGS

Last night I loved a man without asking for anything. To live again, an infinitive. Emptied and dumb-faced. I'm still there.

To make love with him. His offer, a first.

What happens. I can't manage to do anything and I've come back to start again. My body doesn't respond. I'm afraid.

Watch out. Don't lose out on anything now. I've discovered this since I left, as if I were filling up with everything and nothing.

I saw once again the forest and the sea and the strength to encounter myself.

I start dreaming again.

I know what I should do, but I'm waiting for his call. I can't help it.

I've cut my hair. It's time to go.

The night with him is more than a memory, just as his words are hooked deep inside me. I loved him and would have liked to have loved him more.

Yes, I know I must seek myself, but why not give myself a break if I can. Can I?

I've bought his books, I don't want to wait.

Tonight I was thinking: the dominant thought equals the love object.

A necessity, for me or for everyone? Yesterday's emptiness. Went to his house. Finally I thought that, in any case, it was best to do something, to act. I knew I was taking a risk. I don't know what I would have given for him to have a phone.

In my agitation, I barely saw in the alley a young woman playing with a kitten. She seemed very sad.

I climb the stairs. The door was open, and he was there, sitting beneath the window, as beautiful as a god. He was furious. Deep distress, he didn't even say hello.

He started to say how hellishly hot it was, that he had changed shirts three times already, that he had to go to a dinner and he couldn't wait any longer, and had I seen a woman down below? He went to the window and started shouting her name over and over. I couldn't move.

She comes up. I hear her talking softly to him, she was beautiful. An instant to say goodbye and then I was off.

O.K., I evidently needed to prove what I already knew. Feeling bad does no good, so use the experience, put it aside, take without leaving anything, remember, without asking for anything.

He didn't even see me. We have made love, a powerful night.

And I feel I know him, useless, better wouldn't help.

I know I found his soul that night because my body loved him, felt him deeply. And my body never lies.

I'm in love.

I've lost my reason. It's like watching a duel to the death.

In any case a death, mine.

Seeing which reality. What I saw in him. What I want to see. What I invent.

Living it all over again from the start is no good, I take only what I want.

I'm afraid of myself, it's all I can do.

Hard days. Get him out of my head, out of everything. What else can I do. He obsesses me. I ran into him again on the street. I was with Maritza. He sprang out in front of us on his bicycle. A shock. He was uncomfortable too. How is it possible that I see him as so handsome now. Me and all my great theories about the infallibility of first impressions.

He tried a kind of excuse. "The other day I was really down. What are my two friends up to here?" I hate him. To Maritza, "So you haven't found yourself a man yet, maybe one with a nice motorcycle. All the foreign girls get right to it, but you, you're still hanging out with your girlfriend. Yes, I know, I know, you want to be simple too." I can't stand that voice. Why don't I respond. I can't react. I stand in front of him like a perfect imbecile. I look at him blankly. He doesn't give a shit about my eyes, don't worry. He makes fun of me, of my severity, my judgments. He sees my fear, I know.

It's what I want. Remember, no strategies, and the strength to pay the price, pretend to be loved for this, to live, to go deep with open eyes. The discovery. The delirium of seeing yourself, the revelation. Old useless courage.

For this, the desert, and now the fear of living and of dying.

You don't cast pearls before swine. Of course not. But you risk losing them, and anyway what's a pearl, why is it called a pearl, and, first of all, is the pearl real.

I'm tired. Then he looked at me, the other one. He asked me to give him my phone number that he had forgotten.

I wanted to, I didn't want to, and then a power or an incapacity, I don't know, made me pick up pen and paper.

I, too, want to learn to escape.

Only with love comes knowledge, and always possession, even by myself. Indifference leaves me indifferent.

Blood. Today I stopped dying. The sacrifice is complete once again. It is *Cassandra's* evening. Tomorrow I start again.

I'm still waiting for the phone to ring, but I'm already far enough away.

Will my life always be like this, destroying the love I feel?

Love asks, it wants to touch, to suck, and to laugh too.

To the wise one, "How can someone be loved very

much? By being very powerful and not inspiring fear." As for me, either I inspire fear or I'm not powerful.

Immobility. I'm tired of everything, everyone. The past returns, I don't want it to.

Strength. I raise my head, look around. New eyes, and I look for the cage.

No rest is allowed. I die, lose myself, Rome and its broken promises. I want to leave.

Nothing stops me but the absurd feeling of a phone call that can't lead to anything. A night of love? I would ask for more, he knows it. He doesn't want it, or he can't.

I have to leave. I had forgotten, separation is the traveler's fate.

Yes, I'll leave, I'll go back to my friends. T. called a little while ago. He's insistent, laughing, he convinces me. I'm tired of myself, of my meanings, of my images. I want to play, to laugh, with everything. To enjoy. I'll leave tomorrow.

Here again.

I'm fine, I'm fine. Going out, seeing people. Long conversations with T., a friend. Is there a thin thread that divides friendship from love? Yes.

August 15

It's very early. The beach is deserted, the sea almost motionless. The landing place. The sea always sings different futures to me.

By now this too is my place. I remember when I came here at the beginning of summer, laden with questions, winter in my eyes.

They gave me my image.

I'm sitting the way I was then, my notebook on my knee and my nose in the air, waiting for the wind.

Soon the water will lap at my happy feet.

I leaf through those pages. I smile and think of T. His patient responses run through my fingers. "You're strong and confident. You know what you want." "That's not true," I would say.

"Yes, it's true."

"Your eyes twinkle when you laugh. Laugh."

"Quit being so serious."

"You're always thinking. You think too much."

"You're too determined. Of course you scare people."

"Your eyes are an open book. It doesn't matter whether you speak or not."

"You're too concentrated when you look at someone."

"Even your hands pay too much attention."

"You don't accept, you judge. Yes, even without talking."

"You don't let anyone lie, you don't know how to laugh things off."

"You're a threat, you're dangerous."

"Too smart. As smart as a man. Intolerant, and more stubborn than a man."

"And too much woman."

Then he would say, "Enough talk. Let's make love."

Maybe, for the first time in a long while, I listened at length.

I gaze at the sea. Its smell enchants me, leaves me empty and still.

Water mirror, birds resting.

Lightly the waves begin to move, they tumble along like babies who don't yet know how to walk.

I need truth, a truth bigger than my own.

All summer long I walked along this shore with scores of old women, their dresses caught up in their hands, their faces slowly sifting through the detritus the sea leaves each morning.

I continue to read those still-young pages.

These are my July dreams.

First dream—I was in a hospital because I was pregnant and was to give birth that day, or rather that evening.

I'm in a bed and I see the doctors go by. All of a sudden I uncover my belly and say, "But I don't have a pregnant belly." It was an ugly belly, uneven, it seemed more swollen than anything else, as if it were trying to raise itself up in several places like dough with too little yeast or not sufficiently kneaded. Beneath my left breast it was prettier, rounder. And again I say, "It's not possible. I can't give birth tonight."

Second dream—The first time I dream about my mother as a mother, the woman who understands me and consoles me with love. The dream is complicated. A painful situation. First a school with sick children and then our old country house. I was opening the doors. There was my grandmother and then papà, with some abdominal disease. I go out, and I meet a large woman, my mother. Crying desperately, I hug her and think that the world is dying.

Third dream—I had come to a train station. I wasn't alone, it was as if my mother who is not my mother were with me, a living mother who is a woman, a friend. Maybe there were three of us women.

I was afraid, I didn't know how to get out. On the ground were some gratings, people moving around, but you couldn't tell where the exit was.

Something happens. I ask but they don't tell, they are evasive and then I realize that the woman, my mother, had left without telling me, and so had the other woman. And I say, "You could have told me, you could have told me."

I smile. Later I wrote, "The sea, I'm getting a tan at least, and I'm strengthening my stomach muscles."

I am a woman. Being a woman.

I don't understand. Why the need to be defined or definable, in order not to scare people off, in order to live.

The provocation. L., at the end of the argument, caught in his own logic, tries to get out of it with this sentence: "You don't know women." His tone is that of a great expert. "Power, balls, one woman in a hundred."

I answered calmly, "That's right. But for a long time I haven't met a man who had any either." He lowered his eyes.

Must I resign myself to treating men as if they were perfect imbeciles?

I want to go home and get to work. I'm tired of all these useless words. I'll tell a story, the story of a woman, and Medusa has been waiting for me for a long time.

I was ten years old when I first read about her. This winter I came across the old book of heroes with the date and the signature on the first page. It must have been a gift I'd been waiting for.

I liked reading it at night in my room in the tower. I climbed up onto the windowsill just wider than a chair, the book open on my lap and my eyes running like a shuttle from the beautiful landscape to the pictures that bewitched me.

My world was right there before me, and moonlight moved in at just the right moment. The phantoms of the night jockeyed for the field with the ancient heroes and their lost times.

I don't know if I'm ready. I was struck by her strength and solitude and by the trickery with which they had killed her. I kept going back to her story, reading it over.

Snakes on your head. I wondered why they had to kill you. What was it about your eyes that caused so much fear?

Perseus, the young hero, understands nothing. He doesn't realize the risk he's running. It's a woman, his mother, who invokes divine aid on his behalf. It's a goddess, Athena, who allows him to see Medusa without gazing into her face. Mercury, however, gives him the sharpened scythe to cut off her head and advises him to do it without her catching on.

Strange hero. Too ashamed to succeed to the throne of his grandfather, whom he had unwillingly killed, he chose to trade his kingdom.

In his new country he lived happy and content for the rest of his life. His wife gave him several children who grew up strong and courageous like their father.

It's time to keep my promise. I told myself that when I was grown I would discover why Medusa had been turned into a gorgon. What was her crime.

Make love. Useless, for me, it's tied to my involvement.

T. tells me, "Your feelings don't come out. It's as if your skin had closed pores."

Yes, maybe that's it. I'm trying to understand. But I don't love you. I'm tired of all this confusion. I want to immerse my hands and hang my old clothes on the sun. I want perfume, cleanliness, and full, orderly drawers.

The night with him. So, love has only one face for me. Then, love, a game of tag, the emotion of the cheater, the unknown one, the veiled one, the hidden one. Loss of self. Love is the song you hear once again, it's the fullness of running and then eating together afterwards. Loss without loss, there is no love for me.

The ambiguity, the fascination, the disequilibrium, the not finished, the incomplete, the contradiction. Always something that disturbs, breaks, incises, invites you to enter. I would like to understand.

Need to understand. Going back to T.'s house, I found an envelope with a candy inside. I ask. His laughter. "Why don't you quit trying to understand and just suck the candy?"

I put the candy down, I hope I'll want it later. On the envelope was written, "A tautology for you . . . because with you drinking coffee is sweeter."

The key—the body. Meanwhile to recover, this doctor will help me.

I'm tired of pain. And now this mouth infection, a sign? The kiss, the truest offering.

I keep going back to that night, to the way you kiss.

My meanings, my presumption. I know what it means

not to be able to kiss, not to want to kiss. Useless, there's no sense in finding out why, your why.

Summer is over. It's really time to go home. I hope I'll be smarter this time.

I'll stay away a few days more, at my parents'. Today I spoke to mamma on the phone. My sister's home, too, with her daughters, how wonderful!

They're waiting for me.

September

The peace of this enchanting place. The countryside, the other rhythm. The big house here on the hill and, down below, the still lake recalls the menace.

It's always windy. Outdoors, lying on the grass with my notebook.

I don't remember my dreams. Only when I'm half awake do I intuit shapes, one on top of another. Alessandro is a constant. His image comes to me clearly and impresses itself on me violently. He does nothing. He stands near me, barely touches me, his face serious and fine. He's lying or sitting next to or behind me, I always have to bend over a bit to look at him, but it's no use, he's there and I feel him deeply.

My fantasies must have truly wandered far to get to this.

A possibility never relinquished, I know.

Sunset, gorgeous field, and a sun that comes out before it goes down. The magic light, everything fits together for a moment, transformation. My mind quiets. The struggle against the void that devours me and the joy that grows somewhere, spreads, dies, returns. The smile. And memories, and hands left behind, empty.

So much wasted love. I think of a baby, of bearing fruit, and I smile.

I often forget I've made a choice.

I watch the girls. The smallest one is drawing—a toy chest, she said.

The other one runs up, says she wants to stay near me and the dream notebook, now she's writing next to me. How big she's gotten already. The dog comes over every five minutes, wags his tail, licks me and takes off again. Mamma says that when I'm here the dog and the girls get too excited, it's a mess.

I watch him run happily and I see the other one was abandoned and the stone house across from the woods, the unfulfilled dream.

Free to die at last.

I watch the girls. Go outside myself. To kill pain is always, after all, to kill something.

It's cold. Mamma calls us and off we go to get there first.

Yes, I want to start working. I see Medusa the little girl ever more precisely. However, the rest is scattered here and there like debris after a shipwreck.

The key is missing, but there's no urgency.
It's haste that keeps us from gathering flowers.
Tomorrow I go home.

On a night like this, when eyes are useless, fairies seek the love of humans. I laugh softly. I've crept outside noiselessly. Everyone's asleep.

This eternal sky finds its splendor again here or maybe it's me who finds it only here.

The air is so clear that I can divine everything, even a shadow running quickly down below, disappearing and then coming to a stop, still, by the lake.

I go back a little girl.

September 10

Rome. How beautiful it is. The usual feeling when the train pulls into the station. I recognize this air.

Now, clear projects.

Today the year begins for me.

I'll start with my house, still unfinished. I'll build bookshelves, I'll take everything I need from the country house and throw away the rest.

Thin out, choose, and be done with moving. I'll worry about the country house later. Always sell more, but I can't do it yet, I have time.

And no school, after ten years.

I'll know what I want, where I want to go.

This is madness.

Early this morning, happy, buying some new trinkets.

At Porta Portese flea market one loses oneself, and I met Alessandro.

I was walking among streams of people. Looking straight ahead, my eyes met his. My face and his startled in tandem and in tandem recovered. I, badly, he, in silence, took my arm, pulling me in his direction.

A few steps and everything under control, he. I, my hands were trembling so much, ridiculous. He speaks calmly to me, his voice fine and his face the one in my dream.

We go to see the book stalls. He looks, stops, moves ahead, starts up again. Logical, but I didn't know what to do. His shadow.

I pretend to look at the books. Lost, I discover my terror at losing him. I don't know how to explain this, I'm too distraught to laugh at it. As if it came from somewhere far away and yet it seems I've never felt anything like this before. Absurd.

I went up to him. I told him that I was going ahead, that I had to see some things further on. He looked at me a bit surprised. "Sure," he said. "I'll catch up with you."

I left almost at a run, a huge desire to cry.

His hands that I'd barely glimpsed.

His hands and his eyes.

At the end of the street together again. He talks about squalor, the poverty he sees all around, then suddenly, "Are you going to go on or are you going back to the center of town?" I understood. I answered that I was going home. He offers me his cheek, I even kiss it.

I've been walking for two hours.

I can't calm down. I feel like a violin string.

Grass, the little lake. I'm exhausted.

Because I saw him.

I'm in love with him, that much I know. It's just that he doesn't want me. And I don't want to destroy myself trying to understand why.

But I can't help feeling the power of this meeting. It frightens me, it takes me in its grasp.

He was amazed, too, and for the same reason, I'm sure. And then, it can't be too easy to run into someone you don't want to see. If I think of his face I start laughing.

Has his curiosity already been satisfied?

Better to think of how to get out of it, and don't you dare wait for his phone call, because anyway he's surely lost the number.

Ridiculous, I feel ridiculous.

Evening

I read the book you liked so much, with your eyes and my own.

I have to live you first, so I can free myself from you.

I thought of writing to you, of sending you something. A need to test whether it's true or whether I've invented everything.

You run no risk of getting burnt. You, the observer, you don't get involved. The wise man loses, worse than the guide, the wise man doesn't live.

My meanings again. Maybe you're just fine like this.

It doesn't interest you, period. It's easy.

Defining you would be too presumptuous.

Minute observations, to discover you through everything. Discover you, what does that mean. As if there were something to pull out, to unveil. Are you hiding a treasure?

But it's just this that I don't want any more.

I want to grasp reality, what we see, what we touch with our hands.

A sleepless night. The clarity of these rare nights. Another dawn alone.

Tired of being inside you, no, of having you inside me, of loving you by myself, of knowing you by myself. I am penetrating, eating, digesting you. I want to shit you.

It seems summer has exploded.

I feel as if I've just ended a long convalescence.

It was inevitable, I wanted it. Horrible stomach cramps. A night of dreadful pain like that time everything inside broke apart.

But tonight I was alone and vomiting, vomiting.

At last I cried. It was papà I turned to for help with dying.

Now nothing, completely emptied.

I immobile, everything around me moves. It's beautiful, hazy.

Only the lilting lament of unlived dreams.

Regret for everything that couldn't be.

Two days full of him. The odor of his tenderness stays with me. Ridiculous, it never existed.

The end of September

The great winter is over.

Here's the surrounding space. Wide fields, smells, and the wind. She vanishes beyond the stream.

The future throws itself open, widening little by little. I build steps.

I begin to understand.

The past is dead. I can allow myself nostalgia.

The present is conquered.

Stiffness, rage, pain. Phrases used by lots of people, heard and never understood. So then you rebel, look for new toeholds, and when the last one crumbles, you have to learn, finally, to go ahead on your own.

I had to rid myself of everything. Even the work I loved so much. A teacher with nothing left to teach. A way of life broken apart in my hands. Work, the only concrete survivor of my past. The rest a knot of judgments, challenges, to myself, to everyone, to this broken world and its unkept promises. Rigid so as not to die, I wanted the truth at any price.

Last landing, loneliness, the necessary choice.

Destroy needs, give up everything in order to be true.

"You must have been Brutus in a previous life."

Terror remains.

Seeing could not be accepting.

The guide had discovered she was only a guide.

Finally I found humility, always lost again. I left in order to go back as far as I could, the rebellion of one who continually loses the strength to rebel. A well too deep.

I discovered that giving everything wasn't generosity but only need.

Each time I start again from this place.

With bitterness ever waiting in ambush, my liberated needs that no longer wanted to be renounced. And yet the old force pushing, screaming. The yes of one who has not repented. The courage to live the adventure to its conclusion, eyes wide open. The risk of meeting two eyes that you might recognize. To make yourself seen and to hope that it happens again. "It's not indifference that steals weight from the image but love, extreme love."

The true risk, to close yourself in those eyes, to pretend to recognize them, to invent them.

It is with a level gaze that one discovers worlds. My house is born. Enthusiasm. Doors, my doors, all open and there's not enough time.

I keep listening. I gather my images and I even laugh about them. How long will it last?

I pull strings. I separate, put in order, organize.

The definitions continue, "How different you are, how strange." O.K. Sometimes a wild joy takes over inside me.

I'm no longer afraid of the image other people have of me. It fascinates me. The secret, don't lose yourself inside, a prisoner.

So I'll live with my powers. Destroying them didn't help, doesn't help. Affirm myself entirely, my thousand facets.

One thing is sure. I don't like boys anymore, or their adoring eyes. Ladies and gentlemen, the old queen has returned from exile and seeks a new kingdom.

Meanwhile I play at fascinating the mirror.

Walking in Rome at night, enchanting.

I can't help thinking about you, but I smile. I'll meet you again, I'm sure. Fantasize. I often find I'm seeing us laugh together, our eyes complicitous, about me, about you, about everything.

This is the possibility that has bewitched me.

A good time. I'm enjoying myself. Generosity returns, and enthusiasm. It's not hard, I'm appreciated, sought-after, what more do I want?

I smile, no forbidden desires.

Seeing the hint of a chance to leave, I'm getting organized here.

I feel like those insects that resemble bees. They hold still for a long time, suspended in the air, no more than a light buzzing. Then, all of a sudden, in the twinkling of an eye they're in another place and begin again. I think about the game I loved when I was a child. The idea was to draw connecting lines between all the dots spread out in a white square. Follow the numbers on the dots and an image appears.

The new direction won't be easy.

Meanwhile I listen to myself more. My work on my body continues. It's the only sure thing. The balance between the two parts. Life's funny, once I used to hate this word.

The theater grows distant. Writing, instead, is ever more important.

I'm crazy about this research on Medusa, maybe I like it too much.

Emotional and surprised. I keep on reading old texts and new.

The constant tendency to think of Medusa as a monster, as if she had always been one, and as an adjunct to Perseus, the young hero. Anyway, without monsters how could there be heroes.

But Medusa was beautiful, desired and sought after by many, and of all her beauties none shone more brightly than her hair, or perhaps her eyes.

Poseidon, lord of the sea, sees her, wants her, takes her and, changed into a winged horse, descends with her into the sea and comes up on land. The temple of Athena. Hesiod says, "And with her he lay in the soft field and midst the spring flowers."

Profanation, transgression.

Making love.

So that an eternal example might be made, the chaste goddess, her eyes covered by her helmet in order not to see, transformed Medusa's hair into serpents and decreed that her beautiful eyes turn to stone whoever had the misfortune to encounter them.

Punishment, transformation.

Death will come later. Meanwhile Athena will sculpt that cruel face onto her famous and honored shield and to terrify her enemies will bear before her on her breast the serpents she herself has created.

Two images of woman.

Opposites or negations? There's a big difference. Opposites are positive, they generate the conflict that creates every life form. The power of negation, however, is the refusal of conflict. Law.

I've always hated Athena, now it's time to know her better.

Everything makes me anxious and infinitely tired. I

miss the girls. No more excuses. Now I must go ahead, I have no choice.

Athena refused a feminine role, she chose men's values.

Her practical and cunning intelligence is capable of building and guiding and arriving at a predetermined result. Her reason belongs not to women, who know how to use only one reason, the reason of seduction, and thus invincible they become extremely dangerous.

Our prehistory.

One detail strikes me. Athena always covers her breast with the shield and loves to punish. Yes.

These medical studies interest me, the connections continue, confirmations of so much research. Marvelous.

Bodies that speak by themselves, that finally succeed in escaping the labyrinth of words. Buried stories that often tell of passions denied, emotion that comes forth, that vanquishes.

The language of the body is the thread to follow. If I succeed in following it, it will take me somewhere.

Medusa, no one knows where she comes from, where she was born. We only know the place where she was punished, in the West, beyond the ocean, at the edges of life.

I see her as a little girl with long hair, soft, like her eyes.

This evening is a strange evening. My mind is racing.

Relationships with old friends. The strain of building them.

They pass before me, different and yet so much the same. I look at myself. What was it Alessandro said. "You're too simple because you're at one with yourself." It's not true, I haven't yet learned not to ask.

The risk of not respecting others.

I think about F., about our new friendship. Discovering a person is always the most beautiful voyage. Something is happening. I'm confused.

Maybe I'm tired of all those friendships that aren't friendships. I think I know very well by now what they hide.

I want to have a relationship again, I knew this already. I want one. F. wants me. My fantasies brush against his images. The temptation of a place that I already know isn't mine.

Yet, in spite of our deep differences, I can see myself in him. A single terrain in common, but a huge slice of me.

The need for a referent.

F. tells me, "You have the capacity to observe and intuit. You come to these disciplines in a way very different from my own. Let's use what we know, let's work together." The project. Working together is extraordinary. It enriches me, stimulates me. It brings out all the best in me. Growth, pleasure, the only salvation. A lack that destroys me.

F. offers me this and more.

At the conference I found myself participating, arguing. The old pleasure. A day for lions. Gratification, too much.

F. was watching me. I was there like his woman. A dangerous game. Even for me. Strange tastes, distant ones, have invaded me. Stunned, I recognized them.

I'm tired.

I can't even invent a port for myself.

I can't give what I don't have.

I can refuse to cheat.

I don't want to choose for others.

I don't want to hurt.

I want to live.

I don't want to be afraid.

I don't want to pretend to know what will happen.

I don't want to know anything.

I want to live.

Medusa as a little girl

Medusa was beautiful, with long shining hair and enchanting eyes, she was as radiant as the morning.

I see her, a little girl, playing in the woods. Artemis, the foreign goddess, must have been protecting her. Already chosen, the girl was permitted everything, she could wander in peace indefinitely, even beyond the mountains.

She would pass lightly through all her places. Hers was a wild world full of animals, plants and untilled fields. She loved the grazing lands and the fields rich with grain but most of all she loved the wild fields soft with waters that had once stood there. Often she would remain at the edges of the swamps and lagoons or by the sides of the rivers, seeking ever livelier waters.

In the forest she loved to listen to the visible and invisible beings and to enjoy subtle correspondences, there she breathed their perfumes and caressed their odors. Tirelessly she sought them in their secret places, and wherever waiting in gathering shade, she watched for the last light. Like unexpected arrows the brilliance tinged her with gold and then quickly faded. She would laugh, yes, she laughed noiselessly at the eternal game. In the wood even the wind, her faithful companion, would stay behind longer than usual, captured like a bird by invisible threads. The echo would stay as well, and then she would roll in the mud among the leaves, inside the wetness until she got lost, disoriented, until she forgot.

Hers was a time of eternal return.

The Lady of the Animals led her by the hand at all times. The girl felt her nearby even when, tired of playing, she would bound up to the large fountain, a gelid, transparent pool that made her cry out with happiness.

She loved the Lady, the different one. She was her goddess. She, the foreigner, had lead her into the distant places where borders are confused, into the most hidden wetness, into the earth, beyond the frontiers.

She loved the Lady and carried her inside herself but didn't know it.

Perhaps one day the Lady abandoned her.

She became restless. Something whose name she didn't know had been born inside her, maybe a thought she couldn't understand, one that left her no peace, no sleep. She spent hours walking without stopping and her new, restive gaze would endlessly question things, would touch without caressing.

One night, when the moon already shone high, Medusa came to her old playroom, the temple of the sky, and here at last she stopped.

Standing perfectly still, she listened to the sound. Her heart was beating. She didn't know but she listened, something was darting about, it would hide but then come back stronger and more clear. Yes, she was thrilled, her heart or her feet, I know not.

And thus it was the temple of the sky that received her light step.

That night her dance enchanted the shadows, and all those who could see recognized each other. The music of the woods fell silent but not the music of the earth and sky.

She imagined the star of fire as it came forth from the sea with a sound vaster than the night. The sharp new perfume was calling her.

It was time to go.

Thus did Medusa meet the sea.

November 4

I met Alessandro. For once I behaved myself.

Today a nice day. I crossed Rome on foot. I walked and sweated. To cleanse myself. Tomorrow I leave. A working relationship begins. Two heads. A meeting nonetheless. Working together is a little bit like making love, it makes me start with what's there.

Villa Borghese. Air, sun, good-looking people.

I get to the center of town on the double, and as usual my quick gaze questions. And then I'm off, into the morning piazza, the pigeons and the light of white clouds scurrying off.

I was walking rapidly, rhythmically. A sound called to me. I stop short. It was him, sitting at a table with a friend.

He was dazzling. I go over, say hello. He, after asking me what I was up to, starts talking to his friend again. I sit down, listen, ask him for a cigarette, he doesn't have a light, I go to get one, come back, sit down, listen again. I watch him.

This man upsets me but finally I watch him in peace. Moments. His talk, and then, "You know what I'm like, made of watertight compartments . . . . " I raise my head, a joyful smile, I look at him like this. He sees me, I'm sure, but his gaze doesn't leave his friend, who smiles back at me with a wink. An eye game. Alessandro pretends not to notice anything. He kept on talking without hesitating for even a moment. I lowered my gaze, his friend went back to staring at him.

It was time to go. I took my purse and my jacket. "Excuse me, so long Alessandro." The usual kiss on the cheek and, while I'm moving off, after a few steps I turn and, with a sly smile, "Oh, I almost forgot, thanks for the cigarette!" His baffled face. Maybe he thought I was crazy. I like that. And also, this is the first time I get away intact.

Once more, why today? I'm about to leave, to start something new that is fulfilling me (listen to the word I use), and you come along.

It's living for yourself that's hard. Home again, me and myself.

What a funny collaboration you have. "You'll become what I want."

Very interesting. How is it that everyone is perfectly happy to manage other people and I'm terrified of it? Deep down it's too great a risk, and this surely is no time for warriors. Every pathway has a heart, that's it, you just have to find the path.

I'm going to see my little nieces.

The little one has quit asking for my help, she's getting better. Today, slowly, she came to me. You have to be prepared for anything when she moves like that. She says she has to ask me something. Straddling your lap, her arms around your neck, she looks at you, "Listen, I would like a little sister but mamma says she can't, so I thought you might be able to make a baby." And then, smiling at her sister, "We'll help you."

I laughed.

I wonder if they will be my only little girls.

Stress. My strength used only to keep going.

A desire to let myself go. With a man?

I don't sleep. Strange dreams, the non-existent countries are returning.

I dreamt I had to have an abortion, but then it wasn't true.

Athena, capable and cold, knows where to go and how to get there. With her heart protected, her belly denied, she sees and discovers all trickery before it happens.

She rules time and things.

A tireless weaver, she will not stand to have her sovereignty contested.

Arachne had dared to challenge her. Athena, disguised as an old woman, comes to her in her house and tries to dissuade her. Arachne, immovable, repeats her challenge.

Side by side they begin to weave two different stories. The goddess' design exalts the order of Olympus. The twelve deities of the sky sit somber and majestic upon high thrones and Jove, in the middle, authoritative, is the very figure of a king. In the fabric's corners are four contests and the sad fate of whoever dares to usurp the role of the highest gods.

Arachne's song is different. With her agile fingers she pitilessly braids into the threads and colors the deceitfulness of the fallen great ones as they sought to satisfy their own desires. It can't be denied. Each figure, each place, she traces in evidence. Revealed guilt pulses to life before Athena's scornful eyes and, offended, she tears the too-perfect, glorious work to shreds and beats the impudent woman with her wooden shuttle. Arachne cannot bear this and runs to tie a noose around her neck. Ovid tells that Pallas, upon seeing this, was moved to compassion. "Then live, but hang in wickedness, and lest you be tranquil about the future, the same punishment shall be upon all your descendants." Having said this, she sprinkled Arachne with plant juices, which terrible philters caused Arachne's hair to fall out, and her entire body to grow very small besides. Along her sides remain her slender fingers, which now serve as feet.

All the rest is belly, but from this Arachne—as spider—sends forth a thread once more and begins weaving cloth as once she used to.

Restless, unsatisfied. What is it that's not working. No peace. What do I want. What am I looking for.

The girls' letters distress me. An obsession keeps coming back over and over and over again. I can't help you any more. My world doesn't exist, it's a fiction. A mirage. The desert. Death by starvation. Eyes closed. Mouth sewn shut.

The phantasms are waiting behind the door. I know them. Leave me in peace.

Medusa carries me far away. I've taken down from the bookshelf all the books I loved when I was little. I've reread my favorite fable, the one called "Eyes of Stone."

Today, at the girls' house, I was telling the little one how beautiful her new doll's eyes were. My sister started to laugh. "Watch out!" she told her. And to me, "Don't you remember that you used to gouge out all your dolls' eyes? You wanted to see what was behind them." No, I didn't remember that at all. Instead, I see my hands as they rustle under the doll clothes down to the belly and pull out that strange thing that made noise. All my dolls had empty bellies. I used to like to listen to those little cylinders all in a row on the table and compare the sounds they made.

The belly and the head.

I feel like when during the night you suddenly wake up and for a moment or two don't have the slightest sense of space.

Metis, Zeus' first wife, who knows more than all the gods and all mortal men, will always be held prisoner in the god's viscera. Zeus had eaten her because she was pregnant and he couldn't risk having sons wiser than he.

Athena, Metis' daughter, was born after that incident from her father's head.

Maybe I've found the key for Medusa's story.

Yes. The belly and the head.

The serpent's den. As if I were going somewhere else. I found the portrait a little boy had made of me. It's here with my papers, right in the place of honor. I want to see it better. It still bothers me. My head is a big triangle that points upward. Inside, two big eyes and a very pronounced mouth. The body a scarcely-hinted-at little blob, so little it isn't even as big as the triangle.

A body denied. A body found again. Possible shapes, an immersion. As always, necessity puts your legs in motion even when you thought it was no longer possible.

The need to find another language that lets you say more, one more ancient, richer.

Now I lose myself in shapes

And now in numbers

"The fourth nature is water from stone."

"On a base of three (triangle), there rises toward the point of its summit the pyramid, which is born from the relation of four points."

Not so very much time has gone by since I stopped drawing triangles.

"Four is more perfect than three," stated the Pythagoreans, "it signals the concretization of harmony in visible forms."

It corresponds to the four directions of the universe.

The fruit of the soul

The fire from water

The Tetractis is the sum of the first four numbers (10 = 1 + 2 + 3 + 4). Yes, the perfect femininity.

Home. In front of the mirror with the television on. It's very late.

This film is a piece of shit, even five years later. Law, domination, fear, escape. I can't stand it.

No peace this evening. The movie and now this book.

In English class today we had to make things up. I was asked who I'd like to be. No idea. A total void.

They told me, "You're so complicated!"

It's true. I don't know how to make things up, I don't know how to play. Heavy, and even worse, I explain that it's too hard to explain.

Shit. I need help. I want a teacher. This book disturbs me. I want to run away from something.

I'm losing time.

Learn to lose time.

The fourth way.

The age of three is past.

Conquer the four.

Emotions, control. I've been talking about these things for awhile now. I know my old fear has lessened, the fear that made me talk inexhaustibly with everyone in order to take them with me.

Fear of being alone.

Fear of losing my feelings if I've controlled them. It means the inability to live alone.

Memory, my pride, leaves me. What makes up for it? It's more a refusal to memorize, I realize this because of names. Once upon a time it would have been unthinkable.

I would like to understand. Is it possible alone? I've always thought so, but everyone says no.

I have my doubts. Logical. I don't know anything anymore.

The twilight of the gods has been over for a while.

So many teachers, it's like having none, or all of them.

No sleep tonight. O.K., let's move on. I have nothing to lose. I know that I don't know where to go and that creating a stir does no good. Essence and personality. I shall find an answer, images, visions, presences, certainties of seeing something else.

December 4

I met Alessandro just now.

I'm at the movies, he comes to get me at the exit.

I feel awful.

The film great shots and music. Yes, but I'm not into it.

Will he really come? And what will I do then.

Get a hold of yourself, ask yourself what you want from yourself, from him. I don't want to stay at his house, I don't want to make love, and I will say only what I want to.

I get a terrible pain, what has my body produced. Calm down. I have to remember whether it's the fourth time I've met him. Christ, today's the fourth.

It makes me laugh. The faces of the people around me. They watch me astonished, a disturbed woman who gets up every five minutes.

The pain has passed. I was smart. Power and essentialism in the images. Simplicity. Beautiful. The first half is over. Today, end of my isolation. Happy at last, I decide to go see *Kaos*. First, a nice walk.

I go to the center of town. In the piazza I stop here and there among the market stalls. I see him. I pretend I haven't, as if I hadn't gotten his face in focus, my distracted gaze slipping right over him. I actually think he realized this. Right away he's at my side. He takes my arm as we walk. Today he's like someone who's looking for something. Curiosity, even a little anxious, maybe. As curious about me as he was the first time.

More ugly than handsome, his voice and face distorted, a troublemaker if ever I saw one. Essence and personality, right.

The film starts up again.

I was good. I was able to play. He, with the questions right away. What are you doing, what do you think, do you often go out alone, aren't you with a man, practically everything. I laugh happily, answering that I didn't get my leave from school, that I'm in a crisis in the deepest sense of the word, that I'm by myself, that I'm looking for a teacher.

And he, "Look around you, here are your teachers." Oh sure! very interesting, and finally even I have fun. He kept on talking, a long lecture about how, once faith has been lost, the wise man can be seen only from the throne, and this means him.

His dog has died. He says they wounded him. It must have been a drama. I'm sorry. He had such sad eyes.

He invited me to his house. Today the first day he goes out after a bad flu, he's making soup.

I said I didn't know what I felt like doing after the movie, I suggested he come with me. He refused, movies, always a waste of money. So I suggested he come to get me when it was over. He insisted on his invitation, I couldn't be moved.

He'll come at eight.

The film is over, I'm going.

I'm in the street. He's not here. There's still a minute left. He won't come. Take it easy.

The message – "Being strong doesn't mean being like this, with your fist clenched, but like this, with your hand open."

Five minutes late. I was sure he'd come. Roles and masks. The wisdom you talk about, that's what's not playing anymore, the wise man who doesn't have the courage to go up the mountain.

I want the wisdom of the open hand.

I know the price. It's always been worth it. I wait for you for five minutes more, right, I read the story of the numbers in *Joseph and His Brothers*, and when I've finished I leave.

Second Day

His house, December 4, 1984

They head toward his house without even saying so. She had intentionally turned her back on the little street, hiding the worry in her eyes behind a book.

He had found her like this. "So the fabulous movie is over, was it worth the money? Tell me how much it's worth."

She, taking his arm, recounts the fist episode and looks at him. His answer, "Hmm, it doesn't take much to make you happy."

She laughs out loud. The lights in her eyes shine as if they were crystal continuously breaking. She asks him if he's made the soup.

He – "So what's up with the country house, how's it doing?"

She – "The country house is fine. I was there with some friends just a few days ago."

He – "So why wasn't I invited? Aren't your friends good enough for me or am I not good enough for them?"

She – "I had no idea you cared about coming."

He – "Tell me your friends' names."

She – "Why, you don't know them."

He – "Tell me one name."

She – "Marta."

He – "There. What's Marta got that I haven't? Abruptly the other voice. "I would have liked to spend a couple of days in the country."

They're at the house. As soon as he goes in, Alessandro puts on a record and goes to set the table.

She sits on the chair, lets her head and arms relax, and softly whispers, "But what a bore." She breathes a long smile.

They eat, plates in hand.

He – "I want to go to England to buy a puppy. There aren't any breeders for that kind here."

She – "What's the breed called?"

He – "Don't you know it? The dogs of kings, Great Danes. Legend says that Merlin the Magician . . . "

She looks at him, studies him. She is full of impossible questions.

Even when she listens to him tell about his grief over the death of his dog, she feels awkward, says nothing.

Alessandro clears the plates, changes the record and, sitting across from her once again, asks, "So, you haven't explained why I wasn't invited to the country house yet."

She – "Maybe you should wonder instead why we've never become friends."

She is serious, he's ironic.

He – "O.K., why haven't we ever become friends?"

She – "I'm asking you."

He – "So, once we met and were lovers. But did you want me as a friend or as a lover?"

Her face a glass ball, transparent.

She's having fun in spite of herself.

She – "I'd say that's not the appropriate question, it doesn't address the problem. The second time we met didn't offer a choice."

He – "Why, what happened?"

She – "You don't remember?"

He – "I don't think so."

She – "Really? Let's say you were rather pissed off. I had come to find you. You had to go to a dinner and you had this girl with you."

He – "What was she like?"

She smiles. "I don't remember."

He starts a long speech. She listens, amazed at this capacity. Inexhaustible words that slip as if from the sleeve of a prestidigitator and then disappear. And always, with surprise and admiration each time, she discovers the possibility and capacity many people have to talk without saying anything about themselves. And she thinks, "No, this isn't the objectivity I'm looking for. You need to cheat. And fine, you thought it was best to stall for time, that's it, bringing up the center of town made it easy to meet again. Very interesting."

These thoughts don't sadden her. She's happier. He calls her from the other room. She comes in and sits on the bed. He comes from the kitchen ready to start up again.

He – "But when your friends come to the country house do you make them pay?"

She – "Pay?"

He – "Sure. You don't have any money. It's normal to pay for a weekend. Using other people like this is perfectly honorable. Oh, it disgusts you too much. Yes, so then you could get each one to give you a book, you like books but they're expensive."

She's happy, she looks like someone who wants to see how it will end up. He, his chin resting on his fingers, ponders seriously. Now they're playing together.

He – "Or you could find yourself a man with money and when you come to the window of a bookstore press your nose against the glass the way kids do."

She laughs. They look at each other, face to face, close. He, his voice altered, "But do you have a man who wants to marry you?"

She – "Me?" She listens to her startled voice and lowers

her eyes. Then she looks at him, her face the face of a wanderer looking for shelter, she says why she wouldn't do that.

He – "Tell me something. What do you think? Does a woman today like to be proposed to?"

She – "That's hard to say. It depends on who the woman is." Again she lowers her eyes. "Yes, maybe yes, like the fascination of a forgotten language, maybe even its meaning."

Some moments of silence. Her eyes have turned away.

He gets up to change the record. Music again. He stretches out on the bed, pulling her as close to him as he can.

He – "But what kind of man would you want? The ideal man, I mean."

She – "Even harder. The ideal man doesn't exist."

He – "There! I want his basic characteristics."

She – "Well," she counts on her fingers, "Strong, sweet, intelligent, joy of living, and ready to share."

He – "Ah, this is a rich man, my dear, and not just with money. And don't you care about sex?"

She – "Naturally, I took that for granted."

He – "Why naturally? Intellectuals aren't notorious for caring about sex."

She – "And who was talking about intellectuals? I . . ."

He – "So you'd like a bullfighter?"

She laughs: "Not necessarily."

He – "Not so easy to find such a man but you can try. It's hard to think he'd be ready to share as you say. Do you have any idea what he should look like?"

She – "Yes and no. It's not so defined."

He – "And what do you think about kids?"

She – "Ah, this is a real interrogation. I'm not going to answer any more of your questions unless you give me something."

He – "What do you want?"

She – "Give me my image."

He – "No. It's too soon."

She – "Come on, maybe I'll never see you again."

He – "No. What else do you want?"

She – "All right, your fingerprints."

He looks at her with irony. She, recognizing his vulnerability, hides behind a glass wall.

He – "You're a woman who's afraid, who demands responsibility from other people, who needs other people."

She – "And you're not?"

He – "I've chosen to be alone. I ask for respect only from myself. So then, what's the basic thing about choosing to have a baby?"

She – "Feeling I'm ready, and maybe I'd even have one by myself."

He – "And what about money?"

She – "What do you mean, money?"

He – "You need money to raise a kid."

She – "I don't agree. I mean it's not what matters most."

He – "And on what basis do you choose the sperm?"

She laughs. His questions set in motion thoughts still unformed.

She – "I hope that at the very least it would be the result of a night of love."

The music has stopped. He gets up. From the other room, a voice of polished indifference asks, "If you had the power to force a man to share, would you use it?"

She abruptly raises her head. Silence, then her answer, "I don't know. That's hard. I know I'd like it to happen spontaneously."

He comes back, as the other one now, she was sure of it. Again on the bed next to her he starts talking about his life.

She interrupts him, asks him just what is his life.

He – "I'm an adventurer, that's all. Now I could even get married. Why not? The only values I can find stored up in my memory all come from my childhood."

She – "Me, too. That's why I can't make things up or follow rules just to be safe. I know what it means. I . . ."

He, with one finger on her lips, "You're a romantic." She would like to answer, but he begins to touch her. "It's very late. Why don't you stay here with me? We'll crawl under the covers. It's cold." Silence. Then, again, "To tell the truth, since my dog died, I feel a little lonely. I think about everything I've left behind along the way. And I hug my pillow."

She's lying across the bed. She listens to his hand slowly caressing her head. She wants to let herself go. Her eyes close all by themselves and then open just a little, ever sleepier. She doesn't know what to do. His hand, gentle, grows more insistent. Those touches remind her of waves, tall waves breaking on deserted beaches. And his alluring voice, too, enfolds her as if she were being captured.

She shakes herself and says, "Be quiet a minute, hold still. I need to think. You don't need to convince me. I want to stay here. That's not it."

She questions herself desperately. "I can't leave. I should. But I wouldn't feel any better. So stay and steal this night." And to him, with the voice of someone who has already decided, "It's just that I'm exhausted and tomorrow morning I have an appointment."

He had waited obediently in silence. Now he gets up and says, "If you want, you can take a shower." He hands her a towel. "What time shall I set the alarm for?"

In the bathroom, standing in front of the mirror, she looks at his things. All those jars and bottles, sandalwood bath oil and different soaps. "I'm not sweaty; I'm soaked."

And then she sees it. The actor's gorgeous face, criss-crossed by tiny wrinkles, is hanging on the back of the door. The poster reads, "The Man Women Love Best." She stares at it, her expression alternating. Then, standing in the shower, she softly sings a little tune, " I don't want to think, I don't want to think . . . ."

In the bedroom everything is ready for the night.

She slips into the bed that's submerged in down quilts. "It's like a lullaby." To him, "Won't it be too hot?"

He's getting undressed behind the partition. He joins her. Tenderly he kisses her face softly with little childhood kisses. Then, with his face leaning forward, transformed, he turns out the light. Right away, in the dark, he reaches for her belly. He searches, gropes. She, utterly still, notices his frenzy like an unwilling witness, shattered by the noise he makes like a thief who doesn't care about being heard. Feeling excluded, she needs to hold him, to get close to him. She reacts. She holds out her hands, tries to find him, now she kisses him too. She hears his old pleasure but can't manage to love him. She withdraws. She raises him toward her, finds his face, his mouth. She brings her body close to him and hears him say, "I don't know if I can, I feel so weak." But he enters. She starts to lose herself, but he withdraws, denies himself to her. She would like to scream why. She comes a little.

Now clinging to her body, he becomes almost violent, the desperate thrusts of a man who can't. He slips away. Her head selects images, a tangle as immense as her confusion. But she's with him. She keeps him in her embrace, she caresses him, slowly she asks him if he wants to come.

Images start running again. Together with him in a kind of infinite solidarity she strokes him with her hand. She listens to his little groans, a sound that seems nostalgic, the echo of something that no longer exists, or that never did. It reminds her of Gulnara singing "Will he love me, will he love me someday . . . ."

Then he gets up and goes to wash. Afterwards, in the dark, they lie curled up together.

He – "I still feel weak from the flu. I just wanted to, you know, do some petting. But you're worse than a serpent."

She laughs quietly. "You're so silly."

He chuckles. "See? There it is. Your way of expressing yourself isn't always so nice. But I get what you mean. Of course you are too complicated a woman for common mortals. No, not for me . . ."

She – "So then it could be you." She listens to his voice repeating, "Me?" And something she doesn't understand very well, as taken as she is by what she's had the courage to say.

They fall asleep like this. Later he turns the other way, but she feels him close. She dreams about that room all night, about the two of them together. Everything is the way she would want it to be, and he tells her she's beautiful. She sleeps as if she weren't sleeping, aware and watchful of his movements.

In the morning she hears him get up. It's still early. She allows herself the pleasure of lolling around under the comforters. At home she never does that.

She watches him move. The smell of coffee wafts in. Her mouth smiles, her eyes do not. They're already saying good-bye.

He looks closely at her in passing. He meets her eyes. He stops briefly and gives her a kiss.

His voice from the kitchen, "I wonder if you'd make me a cappuccino!"

She, happy, echoes silently, "A cappuccino." The never-forgotten world arrives without hurting anyone. The present is vanquished. Her lips curve ironic and amused. "A fine present, my dear girl!"

He has washed his hair and now sits on the bed in front of the mirror to dry it.

She finishes her coffee and curls up again. Only her eyes watch him a long time in the mirror. She grasps his movements. Quick movements that nonetheless control, cover, adjust. An absurd tenderness invades her.

His voice discovers her, "But didn't you have an appointment?"

She – "Yes, but it won't take me long to get ready. I won't take a shower."

They go out together. She thinks, "There's sunshine again today." He's already different, an unlit cigarette between his lips, a signal.

They go to the car together, he's asked her for a ride.

They seem calm. They're chatting. They're about to come to the place where he'll get out, she's deeply aware of this.

He – "Listen, why don't you give me that phone number I lost?"

She is driving, eyes ahead, and hard. She invents a serene laugh, "I wouldn't even consider it."

A silence. Then their voices start up again. She jokingly pulls off his mirrored glasses. "I hate not being able to see your eyes."

At the stoplight he gets out. They look at each other for an instant. He, "So see you later." And he closes the door. The light's still red. She follows him with her eyes. At the corner, Alessandro turns, lowers his glasses, makes a face and disappears around the corner.

EXCERPTS FROM HER WRITINGS

December 5

Alessandro came. I went to his house, with him. I couldn't leave. Great. "Give me your phone number." "No thanks," I said.

Take stock of what happened, what he says to me. The pieces all in front of me, I put them in order. Having fit them together, a distracted hand undoes them all and I break into infinite possibilities. I need a point, a certainty. Too often in the void, I'm afraid, I couldn't stand it any more.

Sleep, what a joke.

Yes, good girl! I'm not waiting. One thing is certain, he won't call. I've also learned to condemn myself.

But you make me crazy. You've asked me for my number so many times, and you've never called.

What's different this time. Your dog died.

I can't be myself with you. Your irony and aggression destroy me. Always defending myself.

I recognize you yes and no, and what I see scares me at times.

But if you knew that you wanted me—as far as I'm concerned, nothing would stop me.

I see the two of us on the same road, never side by side, we always keep our distance. You, ahead of me, wink the way you do sometimes, from far away, and I have to run to catch up with you. Then you are suddenly behind me, I barely make you out. I watch you, but nothing happens, you don't run. Only your sneer derides me.

You never laugh.

You don't love me.

Perhaps imprisoned by my own meanings, I throw them at you. Mine or everyone's, my own presumption.

This time, ours, a time without rhythm. Loneliness and madness our freedoms. Faithless, yes, our talent is powerlessness. Love, choked pleas. Even the water in the pond has become a puddle and the sea can no longer be found, only in winter, weary of rolling.

But it still means something to look for your own.

It takes two to meet. I don't know if you want it.

To see clearly, penetrate, reveal, this is what whoever is alone needs.

Strange useless courage. And yours, what kind is yours?

I know that I still want to live, and I also want a man, but not just any man. I want you.

But a man who shows himself, who gives himself.

You don't do that. It's as if you're questioning me, putting me to the test. A possibility. But, instead, I feel used. You don't make love with me. And everything contradicts itself all over again. Are your questions helpful to you or to a chance for us?

You've remained alone.

What is that girl to you, your woman or your disciple. And me, what am I to you.

I don't even know if you like the way I am. Not one word about me. I start to fantasize, invent.

It's incredible, I feed you data to find out if you like my body.

I want to be loved, held, desired.

I don't want to make anything up.

I wander around the house, in my life. Useless, I'm full of him.

I force myself down on the cluttered red carpet, notebook and pen at hand I look at the work that awaits me.

How can I place myself in time's ancient order and let all the notes follow their own sequence. I would like to hear the sound that gathers them ever clearer, ever nearer.

Circles in the water.

Who will give me the depths of the sea?

December 6

Spring has exploded, it's impossible to resist.

Out, out of the house, into the street. I want to meet you, I'm beautiful today. I throw open my closet and get dressed.

I am beautiful. I would like you to see me.

I went out with a schoolgirl who came to town to see me. There's no doubt that she wants me.

Off to the center of town. The sunny piazza, the people, all the tables outside, a holiday feeling.

Gaiety, laughter. I was chatting with the girl as we walked along. Suddenly I hear someone call out, "Hey, Miss." I turn my head and, there at a table I see ugly male faces looking at me. In the middle, Alessandro, but it wasn't he who called me. His expression was somewhere between bafflement and surprise.

I don't know, maybe it wasn't me they were calling or maybe it was. The fact is that they were looking at me. Feeling lost for an instant, I wave to him and move on. I sit down on the steps further along, the sun in my face.

Alessandro answered my wave as if he didn't want to be seen, a fleeting but beautiful smile, he winked.

I felt fabulous. I watched him when he wasn't watching me and he was watching me, too, the girl kept me informed. Ridiculous. Too perfect.

Then the excitement passed. Nervous. How can it be that he doesn't even come over to say hello. I saw him at that table, with those people, he was even fooling around with some girls next to them.

Why do I like him?

Then the police came. Same old story, identity check.

Arrogant, stupid, small. A woman sitting on the ground with a scarf around her head and smoking tobacco looks suspicious. But today it wasn't about that. They had been called because two women were kissing each other in front of everyone. They asked me to move. I was confused.

He comes over, asks me. I tell him what happened and he listens, we talk about it and finally he says, "Funny, you have such a normal face." What a bore. "Maybe not for everybody," I answer, but he's already moving along. I feel awful.

A little while later I see him come back. Standing in front of me, he stops, scrutinizes me, and then, "Now that I look more closely, I have to tell you, you have a really sinister face."

I start laughing but he's already moving off, I would like to stop him, to keep him here. I toss off some words in his direction, "Yeah, you're such an expert observer." He barely turned. "Yeah, I know." He was sad.

I just can't live between parentheses. I'm tired. Tired of staying on the threshold. I want my place.

I'm tired of affirming that I exist.

I don't want the mirror.

When the old fantasies are used up, reality advances, shadows flee. What a shame. The shadows are beautiful and reality is not.

Medusa in front of the sea

Alone in front of the sea Medusa is afraid.

The Lady of the Borders had led her to those shores, to the last house, where water and earth blend together and penetrate each other and there she had left her.

I don't know how long she waited on those shores. Surely time began to mark her. Time was running in her veins, in her skin.

Time that slips away and takes away.

Evening

Maybe even he is inhibited by my being, inhibited as a man. Even he needed to tell me that I'm complicated.

Start looking for myself again. Sooner or later I'd discover my essence, if only I'd stop looking for it in other people.

I was thinking about monsters and serpents.

Where there's a monster, there's treasure. The monster is beyond measure, rules the underground world, the abysses. The monster is born from the wind and the water, like man.

The serpent is the soul of the universe, the spirit of all the waters, and the rainbow is a thirsty serpent who drinks from the sea.

On the mountain the flung arrows do not trace rainbows. Questions.

The rose gets lost in the brambles. The ever-wider space reaches out like a spot of burnt stubble. Blurred borders let one bide one's time. I don't know how to wait.

I don't know if summer will come. Loneliness alone does not forget me. I penetrate love, it doesn't bloom. Even death has no meaning. Winter returns.

Medusa is still in front of the sea.

Each evening at night's light the dance begins again. It is slow, the dance of the night. Ecstatic, the world's guardians slow its course but the Secret Lady, even though she dances for her, says nothing.

To the Lady of the Animals and the Mountains

Secret Lady who leads us to the other shore thus do I greet you. Condemned to choose I shall end my prayer, my song. I know not why you have abandoned me but I shall find out.

It's time to go to work again. Here among the papers that await me, Medusa of the sad destiny is born.

I have succeeded in getting the image of Rodin's sculpture. How beautiful is its ugliness. Without unity. Only her body really prays.

Yes, this is my Medusa.

December 7

I shall live the questions. I'll burn anxiety in incense, I'll flood my house. My hands, I'll work the clay, yes, too often they're folded in my lap. My hands have always saved me.

The goddess stories are so beautiful, I never get tired of them. And the hymns. I was struck by the symbol of the pomegranate, I didn't know. Whoever tastes the pomegranate seed cannot help but return. Persephone, for having tasted it, will spend a third of the year beyond the tomb with her groom who this way managed not to lose her altogether.

I've spent a lot of time in the pomegranate garden.

December 8

Curious. Today is a curious day. F. is coming for two days of the conference.

December 10

It happened again.

Collaboration, friendship, don't work if you want different things.

So why not say it. Why this need to destroy myself.

The key word now is not rigidity but immobility. It could even seem like a step forward.

Understand my reality and my responsibility, but also the problems others heap upon me. Divide, separate, don't confuse.

I and my convictions that bother people so much, the violence of whoever thrills you and the need to murder yourself, I know it already.

Yes, I want to be respected.

That time I pulled out my first tooth. A little girl standing on the chair in front of the mirror because I wanted to see. Papà tied the string. I was terrified. We had agreed that, as soon as I was ready, I'd give the signal by raising my arm.

I just couldn't do it and papà, with his reassuring face, was waiting with the string wound around his fingers. I was watching him and myself with my mouth open, I shook my head hard. I knew I had to make up my mind. With a fine laugh, he was saying, "Oh come on, make up your mind." I still remember the solemnity of my gesture and the heat in my mouth and the deep joy that invaded me.

Everything was different then.

Life's funny. There's Alessandro a few steps away from me reading out loud, for my sake, a poem about a little girl.

A December of promises. An invasion of sunshine against the winter.

People flow before me as if they were charmed. This piazza is enchanting.

I feel so strange. Sad? Lonely?

Once again I no longer know anything.

It takes very little for me to lose everything. My fragility. I keep on losing myself in other people's stories. I keep on looking for unity. Who am I, what do I want—the impossible search. I always want to give up, but I don't know what that could mean.

You can't go back, I've always known that. But I'd like to close my eyes. A feeling created and consumed by itself. Definitions, a need, a trace, the spider web. Devour, take over the other. Consume the image you use to live. You rebel. I'm not like this, I'm not only like this. Only separate cages, in rows. Grasping the bars, I can barely see her, down at the very end, screaming like me, like the other women. We take turns going out, the way you want me. Easy, all you have to do is go out alone.

Where have I seen this bewildered woman figure before, her hands full of rags as she wanders about gathering up the ones she drops?

Medusa, fear creeps into the heart of whoever does not know her own destiny, and the crystal mountain shines hazily too far off. All is hidden in this world and we know only what we see.

The sea stretches out endlessly, always the same. Her eyes ache from staring at it.

I've been here so long. Alessandro leans from the steps of the doorway beside me, looks at me intently, asks if I liked the poem. He's talking to a friend, tells me, too, to move over, the sun is going away.

At home, it's evening.

I've come out of it. I smile, I'm waiting for his call. He wanted my number. When his friend went away and he was sitting next to me, he looked like someone who wants to know, as if in spite of himself he were being forced to argue something over again.

Today he wasn't provoking me.

He said, "When are you having me to dinner?" "Whenever you want." A moment of silence then he asked for my number. He kept his feigned-humble eyes hidden behind their lids. I laughed, "I'll give you my address." Then he looked at me. "Your phone number starts with five, right?"

Alessandro had a phone two years ago.

If you don't have a phone you can't wait. You obviously have to act.

But this evening I let my thoughts roam.

In bed I opened this paper I never buy. The signs, invisible traces. In front of me, today's poem, "For Nika," the little secret queen, and I think of the other one. She, too, was a queen, the queen of the woods.

She knew loneliness and strength. Her long walks in the woods and the flowers, the cyclamens and violets, and their time.

The forts and the cave, and the secret smell. The stones and the tower at the top of the mountain, at night, with the moon up above. The peace of the lonely tree on the hill and always the water. Her wet feet and the springs and the clay in her hands and the forbidden river with the little quicksand beaches. In the big garden, the hours of the pomegranates and the dripping, sticky red juice. The walnuts, shaken down before they ripened, September was always the taste in one's black hands. And the wild fruit, full of vitality, and the mandarins that never ripened. The cherries were precious earrings and the grapevine, the fascination of verdigris you couldn't touch. The dawns and the wheat, the ripe stalks that satisfied your hunger. And the times of the garden. The animals, the dogs and the races in the sunshine and rolling on the grass. The always-broken bicycle and the swings put in everywhere so you would always find them. And the big silo, so tall, with its narrow little iron steps, and finally the terrace that you always had to get to. At sunset the pathway was the slow walk to the big oak that invited you to come in. The cabin. And the huge night.

Everything always ended and always came back. The sun, the moon, and their different domains.

The little girl knew what to look for and how to do it. Joy renewed like the first time.

Your place, how simple enchantment is!

With the others, it was another time. They did not understand. Nothing was revealed. Wild games and contests with them, blazing faces, and sweat.

My grandmother always came. She taught me everything. A taste for making things by ourselves, the pleasure success brings, and the love she put into everything she did.

Papà was the time of the wheat. At dawn I'd hear him come downstairs. He'd open the door softly. "It's time," he'd say, and I'd jump happily out of bed and hurry down from my tower. In the kitchen, nonna would already be busying herself at the stove. Mamma would still be sleeping. The three of us and the big cups of milk and in silence from outside the first sounds of the new-born day.

For papà questions were always sure answers. In the middle of the fields, on the machines, he would listen tirelessly, decide, and then take off again. Even the meal afterwards had a different taste.

But the woods were something else. I always went back there.

It was magic.

Endless secrets to learn, places to discover. The damp, the noises, and the smell losing itself in the body, and the searching hands, and the presences. The woods are slow. You have to move quietly, without noise, in the woods. You have to listen for a long time to understand them, it's the eternal thank-you for just being.

Mamma, on rainy days. She was always reading. We used to read together. Her mystery, the hardest one. Mamma was like the woods. She didn't want me to go there, she was afraid of the woods, I, of her pain that wasn't pain, as subtle as a betrayal. Later on I discovered her dreams. Sleepless nights and the complicity of eyes, "Did you like it?" And I, "Yes, a lot."

Your touches. That time I burned my whole hand on the iron, you took me in your arms, on the big chair, and cuddled me forever. Your voice rocked both of us, as if it could be like that forever. An island.

I always watched your face.

I was still sleeping with you. I remember the three of us playing together in the big bed. Then something happened. You left, you were joking, but not really. You lay down on my little bed with your legs hanging out between the bars. Papà was laughing, but it wasn't funny.

Their love was so simple, yours, always denied. But laughing with you was like water coming through a dam. It was papà who didn't understand, but he didn't really worry about it.

I'll never forget the game.

It was a strange game. On some holiday, in the afternoon, all your friends came over. You were laughing a lot. All of a sudden you shut the front door with the chain to hear when nonna would get back. We kids were all taking part in this strange euphoria. The men were all together in the living room. The women were shut up in one of the rooms. The idea was to guess, and whoever guessed wrong had to do something, had to take off a piece of clothing. I was with you and then you sent me into the living room, so I could find out what the men were saying and who was saying what without being seen. You were laughing brightly with your friend. I came back right away with what papà had been saying. Your face fell and I saw you cry softly . Later, a painted smile. You were as beautiful and distant as the lady in the fairy tale.

You gave me doubt.

December 11

He called. Fear departs.

Now I'm going to his place. Even on the phone it's the same thing. He teases me with that voice and then all of a sudden he changes, asks me if we can get together.

How can it be, this is what that nagging feeling is, he's never called me by my name, never.

THIRD DAY

His house, December 11, 1984

She, on time, climbs the dark stairs, led by the music and the light filtering down.

The door is ajar. She stops for a moment on the landing, brushes her hand quickly across her eyes. Her face is tired and tense. A deep breath and she pushes the door open. He is not in the room. Motionless on the threshold, she casts her gaze around. Her eyes move meticulously. She calls him, and right away his voice tells her to come in. He quickly appears in the doorway with a dripping old rag in his hand, the arms of his heavy red sweater rolled up, "I'm finished, I'll be right there."

She slowly takes off her jacket, her gaze fixed, gently bites her lip. She sits on a chair. He comes in. He picks up some papers from the coffee table. He talks about a trip, he has to decide whether to go to England to get the puppy or to Turkey. He moves rapidly. He's nervous.

He asks her what she wants to do, she doesn't know. He sits down in the other chair, looks at her. His provoking voice starts the old game.

Lines like questions that need no answers.

She, bewildered, looks at nothing, without expression.

He – "You don't like me as much as you used to."

She doesn't answer, she's tired. She lowers her head and thinks, "The ice king's back, he's come to get me."

He gets up from his chair just enough to take her by the hand and pull her toward him, then, calmer, he starts talking once again.

She, sitting on his knees, answers without answering, stops his hand as it begins to touch her, defends herself.

He – "Why don't you take a nice trip somewhere?"

She – "Maybe I should."

He – "How do you like to travel, with lovers or with friends?"

She – "It depends."

He – "On what?"

She – "On the situation."

He – "Yes, but which do you like best?"

She – "I don't know, they're different. And you?"

He – "I travel alone. That's the best way, and it's the best way to meet people. Mostly people you never see again." He chuckles, she doesn't.

He – "So you could give yourself a break and take off at Christmas."

She – "Yes, I could, but I don't know."

He – "Hey, come up with a good idea for a trip."

Astonishment in her voice, "With you?"

He – "No. If I like your idea, I'll use it myself."

Her face, like that of a child who runs to open the door but finds no one there.

Useless, time goes by. Suddenly he tells her, "You're a strange woman, you rationalize what you shouldn't and don't rationalize what you should. You don't have the slightest idea where to go. You see something move and you're off and running, but you do it by chance. You've stayed fresh but you need to love too much."

Bitterness in her voice, "Great, you've understood everything."

He – "I really haven't understood anything." He gets up all of a sudden, moving her away. "Let's go to the movies."

In the street the night is beautiful. He talks about eternity. Eternal man, angels who have no sex, no needs. "For sure they didn't eat, didn't shit."

She, her arm in his as if she were attached to something irretrievably lost, walks in silence. She remembers the boy who was hitting balls against a wall. Elegant, racquet in his hand, he hit the balls obediently, ably, deliberately. So he could learn how to play or how to win, she had asked him.

In the silence she looks for other accordances. The still moon is like a sun that's been put out but still smolders. It's impossible to ignore it, their eyes constantly rise up toward it.

He – "What do you think I am?"

She – "The eternal man."

Now he, too, falls silent.

They've almost arrived. His voice, soothed, asks, "Today I didn't see you in the piazza. What was up?"

She – "I don't always come."

He – "But today the sun was fabulous."

She – "Today I was busy."

The movie has already started, they decide not to go in. Back on the street. A lot of people are out. A young woman is walking just ahead of them. Extremely thin, her shoes worn out, she walks as if she were continuously spraining her ankle. Her make-up heavy and as tawdry as everything she's wearing, and from her deep and darting eyes, a strange sweetness.

They watch her. The girl, not paying attention, runs into her, but she manages to catch herself just in time by reaching out. For a second the two women look at each other, smile together almost without stopping and turn around again happy. She murmurs, smiling, "that was close!"

He asks, serious, "What's it like for you to meet women who are different from you, deeply different?"

The smile disappears quickly from her lips. Overcome once again by the impossibility that makes her mute, "How do I experience it—anger and pain, and tenderness, and envy too." But she can't say it out loud. She looks at him, "I'm sorry, but for a while now I haven't been able to talk."

He – "Yes, I'd noticed."

Quickly now her smile returns, and she lets herself be overtaken by the movement, the noise, the people, the stands, the atmosphere of the coming holidays. He buys some nougat candy, says hello to people.

Past the piazza, the same voice: "What does it mean to you to meet someone, what do you think about how a man and a woman experience each other today, and why do they choose each other?"

Mountains rise from the sea. She is surprised, exclaims, "Always more difficult." But he, concentrating, continues, "What do you think of guys who choose any woman whatever just to have a cunt around?"

She – "The cunt, if only it were true, the cunt idea."

They're on the landing. He's taking out his keys, he stops, looks at her, and says, softly, "Yes, I agree, I agree."

They go in. He asks her if she's hungry. She says no. Tired and heavy, lost to the world, she wonders what she has lost. She would like to stretch out and become a part of the earth. She sits across the chair, her head on its soft arm, her legs dangling.

He – "And women?"

She – "Women have lost, at least my generation has."

He – "And the younger ones?"

She – "I don't know, maybe it's different for them. Maybe it's like it once used to be, perhaps they're stronger, I don't know. With new territory conquered, they know how to play the old game better. Maybe they die less. Maybe . . ."

He – "And your generation?"

She – "They don't have very many choices. Alone. Or maybe a man to train, dominate, I don't know."

He – "Wait, tell me one of their stories. I'll be right back." She, left alone, lies back again across the chair. She closes her eyes. They come at once. She calls it the dance of the little clay statues. In the dark, formless, the first one slowly draws near. In silhouette, it lights up for only a moment and slowly fades away, falls apart, dies. And right after that the second one, and on and on endlessly without stopping. They never cross each others' paths, like evening colors before you fall asleep.

The music comes, she opens her eyes. He's looking at her.

She – "Alessandro, I'm sorry, I can't do it anymore."

He – "You feel O.K. in this house, you like it." It's an affirmation.

She – "Yes, I like it." She looks at the window. "I don't know if this is a place where someone could always feel O.K." He, the same look as before out at the front door. He goes back to the kitchen. She, alone again, starts to follow the last trace, and translates the old images for him.

"I lived near here. My grandmother's house was huge, a long, long hallway broken only on one side by endless doors and rooms that were placed one after another. There was never any sunshine except in the big room at the end that looked out over the piazza. I was born there. It was mamma's house. Sometimes I would perch for hours on the high window sills to gaze out. I had to go to middle school in Rome, and even if our country house wasn't so far, papà didn't want me traveling every day. 'You're so little," he used to say. I was ten. And so this big sacrifice he made from too much love deprived all of us of too many things far too early."

The other house was cold and dark and loveless, invaded by rules that I didn't recognize, that sprang up with every step like a mine field, and they laughed. They slid over you until you felt all tied up. In the evening, in front of the television, the people who lived in the house lined up in ironclad order. Each person's importance was determined by his distance from the screen. Ridiculous, it wasn't true at all. The first ones were simply conscious victims, they swapped their freedom over and over again every night for that stupid spectacle. Not even as dignified as slaves. Yes, then I knew powerlessness, and later, rebellion.

At home, though, television time was sort of a party, a running around, moving, opening the deck-chairs. Papà had the big one that would break from time to time. "Because you fall into it like a dead weight," Mamma would say and he would furiously shout that it should have been thicker material, ten hundred times stronger. We would stifle our laughter. And then he always hit his head on the low ceiling in the store room. But papà never let any of us laugh at him when he hurt himself, so we were all ready to burst, we didn't dare look at one another. The ban didn't last long and in the end those evenings were the times we had the most fun.

Mamma had her easy chair, nonna, the chair by the table. "Leave me alone, I'm more comfortable like this," she would say. My sister, the little deck-chair, and me, the low stool. But I preferred to stretch out in my papà's arms with my dog, who followed me everywhere. We would fight for room, he was as big as a lion. Finally we would get settled, mamma's voice saying, "All right, that's enough," and papà's, "Come on now, hold still."

Her eyes, dilated, focus once again on the window. "Alessandro, my world didn't exist any more. I was a foreigner who didn't understand the languages. Everything scared me. Suddenly I was someone different. I began to love the alleys. Long walks in the shade, the silence of steps and the noises, the alley noises are beautiful, and stopping in the lit-up piazzas that open out in front of you all of a sudden.

Then everything changed. At at once I was beautiful and another world began to reveal itself. I fell in love. A feeling I didn't hide but, it was something you just didn't do. My friends, all of them, were stunned at first, almost distrustful, and then I became a precious, fragile thing that shouldn't be sullied. A restraint, the first cage to abandon.

He ate in the kitchen. Now standing in front of her again, he scrutinizes her. "All in all, you don't make me happy. You don't tell stories and I like people who do." She smiles, he continues, "I can tell you hundreds of stories. And even my own." He sits down, his gaze doesn't leave her. "I ran away from home when I was thirteen and ever since then I've lived everything that happened, as soon as it happened. Wherever anything moved, we were always the first.

In all the world, from the first rebellions in England to all the avant-garde movements, always, we were there." His voice is ever more tense. He holds a cigarette that's gone out between his fingers. "We found money however we could, even by taking out some thirty-year-old woman who wanted a little company, old ladies we called them back then. Over and over again, all the time. Do you remember that Ricky Shane song?" His eyes seem almost black. "Then I began to wonder. Intellectuals had confused me, especially intellectual women. I stopped. Now I'm forty and here I am in this house full of books. Sometimes I'd just like to throw them all away. Maybe if I'd kept on with that other life I'd have written some myself." He stops, lights his cigarette.

"I don't regret this choice, it's a choice. I'm still a teenager at heart." She interrupts him, "Are you sure?" He, "Yes, absolutely."

She gets up, takes the tobacco, concentrates on the cigarette.

She listens to his voice explain what it means to have a young spirit. She concentrates on her hands.

Suddenly his voice, "What do you want from me?" She, "Nothing." In the silence their unease grows. Her face is very pale, seems eaten up by her eyes. She tries to patch things up.

She – "Did you like my answer?"

He – "I've heard better."

She – "Alessandro, it's just that you want to play alone, and I want the two of us to play."

He doesn't answer. He gets up, turns off the stereo, goes into the other room. Then the sound of the TV and his voice calling her. There's a good film on. She says she's coming.

On the bed, he's lying down. She curls up next to him. Together they watch the images flit across the screen, saying a few words to each other now and then. Now their bodies are stretched out next to each other. He gives her little kisses on her face, takes her hand and puts it on himself.

She obeys. He guides her hand that by now knows where to go, with little movements of his body. The movie is over. He gets up. Gets ready for bed. He asks her if she's staying, it's a question, not a request. It's two a.m., she quickly thinks it over. She doesn't want to leave. She asks if she can stay. He answers yes from the other room.

Next to her again, he has her touching him anew. She, a car that needs to be pushed in order to take off, he, the push that comes to a stop.

He opens his eyes halfway, "How are you?"

She a grimace, "Well . . . "

He turns out the light. They undress in the dark. Her hands caress. He seems to be taking on something that won't succeed.

They don't meet. Far from each other in their absence they fall asleep.

In the morning he gets up silently. She's awake but doesn't want to be heard. She moves quietly. Her body tries to find the position it held during the night, the warmth. "Like when I used to pee in my bed. When I first woke up, it was lovely, but as soon as I moved, ice."

Calmly she follows her dream, gathers it up.

She lowers the comforters a little. He walks by near the bed, looks at her, and without stopping, from the bathroom, "Good morning! You sleep well here, the sleep of the just."

She laughs. She remembers the phrase that had struck her so strongly. An evening of chatting with an old friend in a winter now long past. That evening the words were strung together like pearls and danced like partners of fire spirits. She, strengthened by ancient passions, advanced resolutely, and grew stronger. Impossible to stop her. Finally her friend fell silent and she, a new, long-speared Amazon, her eyes shining and her breath still heavy, ceased, satisfied with the order that had just been established. Her friend had looked at her for a long time and then the sentence, "Fortunately you have a deeply unjust face."

She jumps out of bed, a nod and a smile for the mirror. To him, loud, "Alessandro, you remind me of a friend."

He – "Oh yeah? And did he try to have you?"

She laughs spitefully, "Of course, he . . ."

His voice interrupts her, "You mean they all try to have you? Well, you certainly are a woman . . . ."

She doesn't catch his last words. She is deeply troubled, she'd like to explain the misunderstanding. She goes into the bathroom, looks at him. He's fixing his hair in front of the mirror, moving his lips ever so slightly. He smiles at her ironically and kindly. Far away.

She leaves the bathroom without speaking. She finishes getting dressed.

They go out together. He takes his bicycle. "Today I have to get my driver's license."

She's surprised. "I thought you didn't have a car."

He – "No, I have a car, but I don't drive it."

It's still early, the air is cold and dry, and the day appears to be splendid. He talks inexhaustibly. She tries not to listen to him, plunges herself in the noises of the alley that's just waking up.

They head for Giolitti's. By now it's a ritual, like his useless words. "Your old boyfriend used to do a hundred kilometers a day on his bike. Now there was a real man!" A silence then, his face distorted, he continues, "But clever lads like me are often impotent!"

She doesn't speak, her lips dry, like when she wants to make love.

Leaving the bar he asks, "Where are you going?"

She – "To see the Chagall exhibit."

He – "I've already seen it. If you want I'll tell you the story."

She – "Yes, I'd like that."

Standing on a street corner, he holds the bicycle with his hands. She, one hand on the handlebar, looks into his eyes. She listens and doesn't listen. Stunned yet again by his transformation.

And that clear light that penetrates her reminds her of the color of the sea when from high up it seems to collect in little coves. Almost always unreachable, the coves shine more brightly from up there. Still and deep like children's paintings.

She makes herself pay attention.

The story is over. A little smile, a playful thank you.

Alessandro gets on his bicycle, touches her cheek with his own and wordlessly takes off.

EXCERPTS FROM HER WRITINGS

December 12

Just seen the exhibit. Struck by Adam and Eve, two bodies in one, *The Love Story* and its meanings once upon a time.

Sitting on these stairs I and my notebook, my reality.

Another night with you.

It's true, I'll go after anything that moves, but the fox I hunt doesn't run away and knows what it will cost him if he does. The Little Prince didn't understand. "I don't have time," he said, and she, the fox, gave him the secret, "whatever is essential is invisible to your eyes." The color of wheat. Who knows if you know it.

You're right, I need to love. You and your truths and questions and arguments. Games and more games without ever playing. A fearless courage. Right, the eternal man.

I don't know how to define the way I feel. Calm, slow. No, it's not fulfillment, a knowledge.

The dream. You and I were in a house in a town that doesn't exist. It was my house, and it had been closed up for a long time. It wasn't the country house.

We go in and you weren't yourself anymore. You moved around and talked like a transvestite. The house had a penetrating smell, as if some dirty clothes were stashed somewhere. It was in the bathroom. A white nightgown, very beautiful, that I bought for my first important party, when I was sixteen, I made a gorgeous evening gown out of it. I was beautiful and I loved being beautiful.

The nightgown, all dirty and crumpled, was carefully hidden in the bathroom. I don't want you to find it, but you go right to it. You see it, you tell me someone left something dirty in the house. I don't answer, I know I did it. I don't say it. It was as if, a long time before, I had shat on myself and hadn't had time to clean up. Afterwards it's only me, kneeling in front of the tub, like when I used to wash the girls' diapers. I can still feel the cold water in my hands and the shit in pieces, crusts, coming down.

Behind the big fountain the water was stagnating. I used to like to dig into the slimy clay and watch the water spread out fast into the furrows I had dug in the earth. Like the marks of dry branches fallen from the trees in winter.

And the water began to flow again.

And the future neglected the past, the pasts like crusts on dead water.

Evening

It's useless to believe I know you. Now I even love you.

Medusa loves the sea

Sea divine to look at, I want to close my eyes and breathe the deep water of your abysses.

I'm tired of scrutinizing the play of the waves, I want your belly heat.

The bottom of the sea. You have to immerse yourself without being afraid, it's the descent necessary for life because the depths shine higher than the sun. Perhaps the stars gleam even there, perhaps even the bottom, scratched by limber, expert hands, hides the seeds of fire like the seeds of a pomegranate. And perhaps the roots of the mountains and the green, the perennial green of the grass.

Night

Immersion, abandonment, surrender. Trust, yes, but what, nothing.

Because I want to hide my shit from you.

December 13

Today there's no sunshine, I wonder if you'll call. Time runs through my fingers. I am incapable of transforming it.

These words an obsession. "Do you know where my strength comes from? I have never been loved."

No one pays my ransom. An unbreakable spell holds me. A hundred turns . . . the circle.

Let me go.

December 14

I struggle, I struggle. Nobody. Whom should I seek.

The great past, like exile, helps you. Refugees are so sad.

I want to come into this time. With borders, my own, accepted. And all my memory. And I want exchange and to come in again to your, to my garden.

It's magic says the little girl.

I have to get up it's almost night.

It's just that when I leave him everything seems over and it's never true. Fragments have been pruned onto me and I can't tear them off. In my hands a stretched rubber band. Forward, back. Wait till he breaks. Pull harder.

Eternal man.

Exhibition and negation. I discovered I was an invalid. Many years have passed since the night I had that dream. I and an old woman, near each other, were looking straight ahead. A very simple room opened as if it were on a stage. In the middle, an iron bed up against a wall. In a corner, almost in front of us, a marble table. And in the back you could make out something like a cradle. I was waiting completely still with bated breath. Suddenly a woman appeared and began to move around the room.

A simple, modest woman. She had long, uncombed hair, black like her large, deep eyes full of pain but unmoving.

Her face was creased, she seemed infinitely tired.

Walking slowly she came to the cradle and with immense care took a very small baby into her arms. She looked at him so sweetly. She looked into his eyes for a long time and meanwhile she was moving toward the table where a closed box had appeared. I, with dry lips, ask what's happening. The woman by my side tells me her story. She can't keep the baby because she's an invalid. It was true. One of her arms hung limp at her side. Upset, I would have wanted to cry out that it wasn't necessary, that she could get help. Terrified, I saw her put the baby in the box. With infinite love she tucked in his head, his hair. Then I didn't see anything else. When I opened my eyes, it was only she lying down on the bed. An old woman, with the sucked-in face and the open mouth of the dying.

Why doesn't the body lie and scream first. Mine or everybody's? Your body, you're killing it.

I love solitude. It's lacking someone that kills you. Only then, alone, do we die.

It's night and I'm still here.

I would like to tell you a story. I can't. Why, why.

Power.

To see is to take away power. I frighten myself, I get myself destroyed.

Impotence.

The courage to show yourself.

The fear of being ridiculous, inadequate, or ancient, as you say.

Why do I want to hide my shit from you?

Your offer.

And I, what have I offered.

Judgment.

The poster in the bathroom, "The man women love most." It must even be recent, the actor's face is very lined. You put that poster up behind the door, you see it only when you're sitting on the toilet with the door closed. But you always close the door.

That poster in your house.

You're too smart not to grasp the absurdity of that phrase and yes, your face could resemble his.

Maybe you needed it when you were taking out thirty-year-olds.

I don't care a bit.

Because I recognize you.

It's not your pain that frightens me.

I'm so tired. Tonight I resemble my mother.

Poseidon

Maybe a god neither too light nor too dark had been destined for her. A god halfway between the servants of the great mother and those of the new father of the gods. His realm was the sea but only because he had married its queen.

December 15

I'm in the piazza but he's not here.

A sleepless night.

The same ending. I'm here.

I have the blank tapes with me, needing an excuse.

Really distressed.

Because of this terrible effort.

I want to laugh, how many people wouldn't recognize me.

I've decided. I go.

I found him on the landing of his house among slabs of cement, pieces of wood, and tools. An invisible guest, I would have wanted to stay there on the chair with the door open and watch him work. He sent me away gently. "See you," he said.

Look into each other's eyes for a moment.

I want to bring him something, he hasn't eaten.

Don't even consider going back there. I'm exhausted, as usual, after seeing him.

Medusa's signs

She feels the signs on her face not on her body which instead becomes freer and lighter. Her face bears weights she can't release. Her head, her thoughts, her pain when evening comes seem huddled around her eyes, her lips.

Not when she laughs.

Evening

I saw the film *Passion*. "What are you doing, Isabel? I'm doing what everyone else is doing, going home . . . . End your story, it was already over before you started."

And you ask me what an encounter is.

No to oblivion and silence

Could I but sing, death's power would leave me.

Precious memory that enchants the silence. Don't trick me.

I want neither praise nor blame nor the glory due great men. Only to sing an old story that speaks of sincere prayers and ancient wisdom.

December 18

Another hell. I need to die so as not to pretend I'm living, who cares, I'm beautiful tonight. These days out of the hold, it's done me good. Joy and gratitude. My friends look at me smiling and perplexed or worried. I don't eat, don't sleep. Invented marvel, who cares, I want to laugh.

The night with L.

Telling about a missed encounter with someone who understands encounters makes you strong, who knows why. A friend who knows you, a companion with whom you can go far. The night fled away happy among masses of words squeezed out and thrown away. It was dawn already when his woman got out of bed. From the doorway she looked at us, shaking her head and L—certainly I won't forget L—drunk by now, standing in the kitchen singing the Nazi hymn with his arm raised.

Clear sensation, when I woke up, of having gone overboard. Who cares. Now I know what I have to do. Orderly reflections. You and me separately. I was confusing things. I unknotted tangled threads. Something distresses me and I can't manage to understand its nature. Why unloved? I don't know, it doesn't matter.

You'll be the one to decide.

I know what I want.

The other day you asked me what I want from you.

I don't know. I want you. I don't know what that means. I know nothing.

A voyage with you right to the end. The only risk that's worth anything. The honest game, the open hand.

And it's you who raises my hand.

Killing doubt gave me this truth.

I wasn't generous.

Maybe I'm not generous any more.

I would like to give you my shit and run to you.

Hold you.

Melt the ice, yours, mine, I can't.

I don't know if you want to.

Too little courage to go up your stairs.

To meet.

Once you asked me, "If you met a man you liked and had the power, would you use it to make him share?" You were thinking about yourself but who were you asking.

And what do you think a woman's power is.

I don't want to force you. I know what I'd pay. I want a grown-up love. Don't ask me what that means, I don't know, but I've seen the truth about something and I need to live it. I can't negate it. I can't go against it and I can't go back. Man and woman can only change radically and evolve or else perish.

A partner, a companion who understands your heart, who can withstand your weapons. Two free beings joined together. A few drops aren't enough for me I want the ocean.

I don't need a man in order to live and I don't want to complete myself, the thought makes me shudder. I don't want to forget my misery but instead reveal it. And if the heat is intense and the pain too great, I have no other place to go. I stay here.

I wander around the house. Medusa is waiting for me and I've got to get back to her. Finally I sit down and look at this photo, the one with the Rodin sculpture. Too black, too much guesswork. This body on the ground, arched with effort, all its muscles and strengths want to hold onto that indifferent foot. You see nothing of her, only the effort. That's probably why you can't find the picture in any catalogues, at the very most they quote its name, not even the Rodin museum has any copies. Incredible.

We have to light up this body, signal it, show it. It can't be opened.

I keep on taking notes.

Medusa looks for the truth that is prayer, the power that guarantees the dawn's return.

Truth acquires all its meaning in relation to the muses and to memory, it's the muses who claim the privilege of telling the truth, of saying what is what was and what will be. And memory is everything, if lets you decipher the invisible, it allows effective words, it is the gift of clairvoyance.

The search for this truth brings us to the riddle, the poet, and the Old Man of the Sea, the king of justice.

The poet is powerful, can manage oblivion and silence, the power of death against memory, the power of life and the mother of the muses. Truth and oblivion tend toward each other, sweet oblivion, sleep, the shining vision.

The wave gave birth to Nereus. They called him the Old Man because he is an infallible oracle and diviner. He never forgets to be fair.

The justice of the sea.

To immerse oneself is the test, it is to penetrate the world of the gods, and to come back you need their assent.

Trial by water.

You ask me about women and you haven't even seen me.

I play with my fear. There's no connection between your belly and your head when your heart says nothing.

Wait. I hate waiting. This is the time for moving, I have nothing to lose. Now it's decided. I'll give you this marvelous book, *Hopscotch* by Cortázar. My power, the only one, is to tell you I'm here. You'll take what you want.

On the rock, my hands holding my tucked-up legs, I look far away.

When it happens, what will it cost.

Prayer to the Old Man of the Sea

Old Man, my mind is killing me and I fail to ask you anything.

I'm restless, give me true reality and not vain images. You who exist before time and you who do not forget, look at my pure body, grant me your wealth.

Sweet Old Man whose voice shines, show me the path, break my sleep. Let memory and oblivion hold up my heart. The pitiless voyage awaits me.

Make me a warrior.

December 19

Hours for discussing strategy and seduction.

Useless, the era of Athena has returned. I can't accept it.

I read the book. I trace the net I'll give you. I have an idea. Cortàzar writes in the table of contents: "In its own way the book is many books, but mostly it's two books. You read the first the way you usually read books. You read the second beginning with chapter seventy-three and following the order indicated at the foot of the first page of every chapter."

I chose the dedication. This phrase has been entering my mind for some time now. I like the way it starts, the first letter of my name, and the way it ends.

I began the choice of themes and the numeration. I'll write, "Third way of reading . . . an answer to your questions at last."

It's a huge work.

I'm very tired. It's very late.

I don't know how to define myself, maybe a witness of wasted desires.

Total themes, that's the key. It seems easy. Maybe the point where everything falls together is missing.

Maybe I'm not ready. And yet I know the seasons, I know them well. Once when I was a little girl they asked me what I would like to have in my life forever. "Clear ideas," I answered.

It makes me smile.

I look at the tense face of Medusa who waits for a signal that she may depart. As far as I know, no woman has undertaken the trip, the descent into hell. I even asked, but nobody remembers anything like that.

Our story.

It's sad, the promised land, the landing place, it's Athena's temple. And order, the true order that allows flowers to unfold, fades into the distance.

How much confusion. Men's stupid laws.

Once she found the courage to go, Medusa is left with the memory, the memory of that night.

His call.

He asked me why he never sees me anymore. He grinds words at high speed. He talks about the Christmas holidays that are coming up, asks if I'm going to give him a present. Finally, with a changed voice, if we'll get together tonight.

I'm here.

Deep night, and it's cold. I've just parked near his house. Rome is deserted and there's a wind, wind.

A strange calm in me as if I wanted to prolong this moment. Now I go up.

Tonight, the closet open, I listened and chose. I asked myself who I wanted to be.

The sorceress. Her incantations. I read today's notes for Medusa.

You have to go further back, further. And first, acceptance, surrender, abandon.

Magic is a conquest and comes after rebellion. And once the mind is changed, the incantation will work on the world.

The sorceress, furious and wise, does not surrender but works. She attracts and uses what serves her, she is the maker, the witness no longer.

Medusa discovers the sky

From the depths of the celestial ocean Medusa sees the six wise ones and the discordant music stirs her to the core.

Her mind now changed, she is about to see.

She laughs and seems to challenge worlds with the power of her pure eyes. She asks for the power of the beginning, of being lover to what she sees and touches.

Dread and pride, the joy of what awaits her.

Revealed forms. Now the sea that contains them all no longer makes her fearful, she is almost impatient to go in, she waits until the sun unrolls its carpet.

The rulers of the sky will be with her.

Fourth Day

His house, December 19, 1984

The door is ajar. She enters without hesitating. "Where are you."

The television is on. He's washing the dishes. He sticks his head out from the kitchen, they say hello. Standing in front of the TV screen, she takes off her jacket and her scarf.

She – "It's really cold tonight."

He – "Yes, I heard. Do you know this movie, it's the story of Saint Philip."

She – "Not really." She watches the images. Her eyes shine, amused. She can't help but laugh at the actor, who has always been a comedian, dressed up like a saint. But he is serious, solemn, he starts telling her the plot. Her lips are trembling and seem to be waiting for the starting signal. She controls them.

The noise of dishes and running water. His face appears fleetingly at the door. She, meanwhile, has lain down on the bed. Languid now, she has a vision. That summer night in the meadow, lying at the edge of the field, she was watching her friend and the little girl play together. Suddenly the child, "Why don't we get undressed because I want to see your eyes?" And he, "We don't need to, here are my eyes." The little girl sighs, "Those aren't the ones, your eyes are here, here, here and here." Her hand runs over his body all the way down to his feet.

The movie is over. Now he's in the room, picking up here and there.

She – "Can we turn off the TV?"

He – "Yes, of course."

A commercial. An eagle soaring in the sky.

He – "Isn't that fabulous?"

She – "Yes, it's beautiful."

Taken up by this, they say nothing. He comes toward the bed, sits down.

She – "What have you decided, are you leaving?"

He – "Most likely I'll go to Istanbul, across Eastern Europe, a part of the world I don't know. As if I were allergic to it."

He turns off the television and lies across the bed in front of her.

He stares at her.

He – "Someone like you should know those places, right?"

She – "Why?"

He – "What I mean is, aren't you nostalgic?"

She smiles, "And what are you?"

He – "I could call myself a capitalist anarchist."

She – "Very interesting."

He – "Have you been there?"

She – "In Bulgaria."

He – "What are the people like? Are they good-looking?"

She – "They're sad, very sad."

He watches attentively, "Tell me."

Little events, impressions, surprises. Her voice, uncertain, is like the motion of a caterpillar.

He – "You like to travel. What are you waiting for, sell the country house and take a trip around the world."

She – "Perhaps."

He – "Time marches on. Maybe it's better to find a good man and have a baby."

She – "I've never liked good men."

He – "So that's why you've never had a baby."

She with eyes half opened – "You're wrong there. On the other hand, I've had an abortion, more than one, three to be exact."

He, surprised, "Why did you do that, you could have avoided it."

She – "Yeah, but it happened."

She gets up, finds her purse, takes the tobacco out. "It never happened to you?"

He – "No, not as far as I know. Did you decide or did your boyfriends?"

She – "I did. I chose."

He ironic – "You denied them this happiness then."

She doesn't answer, with lowered eyes and pursed lips, she rolls a cigarette.

He – "You have to make your investment while there's still time. And by now you don't have very much time."

She – "You know that better than I do, of course."

He gets up, looks at her. "The life I've lead never allowed me to have emotional investments, but if you want to have them, you've got to be stronger than you are. Live fantasies and control them. I couldn't advise you to do it."

He goes toward the bathroom and before closing the door, "I've always told myself that in the second half of my life I'd be able to absolve myself of this task. It's a moral question, you know."

She is furious. She looks at the closed door. "The eternal man has spoken. Task, moral. Shit. As for emotion investments, I've made them all my life, and I've paid for them. You cheat, you mess people up. Security, the horror of loneliness, risking one's ass is something else. I've always taken risks, even for one single night of love. Fuck being a woman. I'm tired, tired of scrutinizing behind the facade."

He comes back into the room.

She, decisive, "Alessandro, I don't like the way you talk. I don't like the way you tell me what I should do. I can't . . ."

He interrupts her – "I'd like someone to tell me what I'm supposed to do.."

She – "It isn't that. It's the way you come on that stops me. I can't . . . . "

He interrupts her again, "I express myself the only way I can, by talking and not talking . . . Eastern style. Combinatorial equations, like the old Chinese fable you tell. Ancient philosophy . . . . "

She doesn't listen, "The fable says something entirely different, useless." She looks at her watch. She wants to leave. "What am I doing still here."

He interrupts himself, comes over to her, a little caress on her cheek, "Want to eat something?" She – "No, I'm not hungry." He, his voice tender, "You never eat." He smiles, "A cheap date. Wait, I'll get some wine."

She looks at herself in the mirror, "It takes so little to get screwed up."

He hands her the glass. "Tell me, how do men experience you?

She – "It depends."

He – "On what?"

She – "On the men."

He – "Yes, of course. I mean in your story."

She – "As a mother, or anyway too demanding, scary."

He – "You as a mother!" She laughs.

He – "Does your head scare them?"

She – "It depends."

He – "Do you like them to experience you through your head or your body?"

She smiles, "That's a hard choice."

He, engrossed, "You demanding. Strange. You're not the type."

She, attentive – "I'm not?"

He – "No. A demanding person asks for things you can't give because of substantial life differences, differences in understanding."

He gets up, turns off the gas heater. She, lying down, looks at the ceiling. He comes to her, moves her toward the middle of the bed.

He – "Let's get under the covers, it's cold." He touches her softly, "The first time we met was quite a night." He laughs, barely, and then, "But tell me, your boyfriend . . . ."

She interrupts him, "Give it up, if you say that word one more time, I'll pull out your hair."

He – "Don't do that, I don't have much left."

She, her face hidden by his shoulder, hugs him tighter.

She – "Alessandro, don't you ever laugh?"

He – "Sometimes."

She – "When you're alone or with others?"

He – "It depends. Make me laugh, now."

They start to make love.

With her clothes on the floor, she looks for his lips and her tongue slowly opens licks cajoles. Her hands softly seek hidden odors. He, still as can be, seems to be waiting. She begins to join him. An obscure strength invades her. In the dark she smiles, slips off his tee shirt, his last defense, and, with changed name, invents herself as a warrior. The fires are all lit. The dance begins. Its rhythm takes her. She runs wild over his body. Vigilant, she touches the strings again before the sound dies. She rouses him, "Are you there, are you there?" She takes in his yes as if it were the last flower on earth. She begins to forget. He is inside her. He doesn't know. And finally water, only water everywhere.

She collapses on top of him. Only her hand still plays over his face. Suddenly she raises her head, laughs.

She – "You see how it can happen?"

He – "But you have your period."

She – "What do you mean, don't you know it's dangerous."

He – "Yes, sure. But I let you know I was coming."

She smiles, "Yes, it doesn't matter, I was just saying it." Her face just inches from his, she stares at him. The little red light filters in from somewhere. She wants his eyes.

He – "What are you doing?"

She – "I'm looking at you, I want to guess your face."

He, with changed voice. "You don't know who I am, right? . . . But I'm me."

She – "Please, no projections. I know very well who I'm with."

She kisses him. They stay next to each other without speaking.

He – "So are you going to give me a Christmas present?"

She – "Of course, I've already chosen it."

He – "Is it something useful?"

She – "I think so. It depends on what's useful to you."

He – "I don't know. A bar of soap or some bath oil are useful. For me, a record isn't useful. For you, since you don't have any, it would be. I'll give you some records."

She sulking, "Why did you say that?"

He – "Because I want to know what my present is."

She – "I'm not telling."

He – "Come on, let me guess."

She – "I can tell you that it starts with 'm'."

He – "Uhh, I'm worried I won't like it."

She laughs. He gets up, goes into the bathroom. He asks her, "Do you want to take a shower?" She, "No, no." And softly so he won't hear her, "I like your taste." She caresses her stomach. Her slow hand traces ever smaller circles and then begins again. "Anyway, now it's done."

His voice again, "Listen, why are men so afraid of menstruation?"

She – "Not all of them."

He – "Blood makes me queasy. Doesn't it you?"

She – "No, not the way you mean."

Together again, in the same embrace, bodies entwined. Their words, light and well-meaning, waft up like soap bubbles.

They fall asleep in each other's arms.

During the night he asks her to move over a little bit because he's falling out of bed. She detaches herself with effort. The cold shadow has already returned.

It wasn't true. Stupefied that the light has come back, she welcomes that body once again. Peace spreads over her face.

The alarm clock goes off. It's early. She's the one who has to go, she has an appointment. He kisses her softly. He gets up. From the bathroom he talks to her.

He – "Did you hear the rain tonight?"

She – "Yes."

He – "It was raining hard, and I thought, I wonder if she feels protected."

She doesn't answer. Immobile, with bewildered eyes, she holds back the chastisement. She gives herself up to the hope that has marvelously opened for her again.

A few more minutes next to him and then she can't stay any longer. She kisses him softly, decisively pulls back the comforter.

As soon as she's ready, she comes over to the bed.

Bending over, she reaches his face. In a whisper, "Alessandro I'm going. Listen, I can't find my earring . . . ."

He, with eyes closed, smiles, "Is it gold?"

She – "No, it's not gold." Tenderly she caresses his hair. "So long."

He – "Let me open the door for you."

She – "No, don't worry, I'll do it myself."

He – "No, you won't be able to."

They're on the threshold. He hugs her and in one ear, softy, "I'll call you."

EXCERPTS FROM HER WRITINGS

December 20

I have to sleep. Absolutely. And later the book.

The Sign

Medusa laughs, she has seen the thirsty serpent drink in the sea. The bridge is down. The seven-colored stairway slides over to her. Death or life she doesn't know. The arc drawn across the sky is the much-awaited sign.

Out of breath. That's it, I'm out of breath. As if I didn't have time.

"I'll leave the mark of a difference," says Medusa to the stars on the evening of her courage, her strength.

December 21

I'm still reading *Hopscotch*. This book reconstruction kills me. I've already chosen the pages and the lines. Naturally, forty pages.

Now I have to sew them together in the new order. Then the finale. "The third way of reading," that is, mine. The answer I didn't know how to give to your questions.

It's no good.

And the La Maga's letter tears me up.

My only desire to stop and cry in peace for Rocamadour the way Useppe did so many years ago.

And for all my unborn children.

It's no good, no good.

Straining. I'll also give Alessandro some bath oil.

December 22

Away with the book, away. No more words. I'll give him a lamp.

Centuries since I menstruated so much. I'm exhausted. And happy.

Incantatory Song to the Stars

Gods, tonight our hair is of the same color.

The nights of time, all of them, have curled up next to me. The shadows have changed, they crumble endlessly like unstrung pearls that roll all the way up there.

After many days all alike I discovered the sky and from its belly I see the fount of all the waters rush forth. The Milky Way cleaves it perfectly in a wide pathway lighter than the rest.

The road is forever the same, traces both above and below, and always the memory of an ancient fear.

Powers of heaven I have lost your names but you eternally rotate in the same place forever. I have time, awakened by the patient roll, my body outstretched, I listen to the perennial motion.

Like a rope striking the floor I seek its rhythm, its beat.

Guardians of heaven how beautiful is this arc of light. Let me enter.

Tonight my memory is a stairway of precious stones, each step has striped my body painlessly, it unwinds as thin as wind between poplar leaves in springtime.

And with hands held high, for only the stars escape my hands, I offer you openings. And my devoured heart.

What's the difference, I laugh, too many hours have I spent in the garden of the pomegranates.

The lamp is fabulously beautiful, just as I wished it. And now the card. Speak and speak not. I think I've said everything, you'll take what you want.

For Alessandro Christmas 1984

I hope the thing satisfies your idea of usefulness. I could have given you some sandalwood bath oil (just to be sure) but that wouldn't have satisfied me.

I think this lamp is really charming, it can be pointed wherever you want, used in many different ways.

I saw it there, behind your bed, which I think suffers from its absence.

The story of "m" still remains.

> " . . . maybe the rose petal dust belongs
> only to the vendor of essences."

Then I drew the hopscotch squares. The spaces with the marker, and a semicircle on top, heaven to be reached. Really it looks like a door. I wrote above it, "Hopscotch"—below, "left-over from the previous gift."

Medusa before the sea voyage

I like an absolute gesture Medusa makes. Describe her from far away when she gets up, smiles and goes down into the water.

Now your big present is there, on the table, next to the little presents for the others. Life is funny. I had a good time looking for the lamp, you'll like it. Will we ever make love with the light on?

Medusa during the sea voyage

Very few words about the trip. There will be only a sensation of lightness, a loss of weight that will go together with the heat that expands and finally the rocks, the beasts, the Guardians of the Mountain.

He telephoned.

You can't feel like crying, you ought to be happy. Come on, he called you. It's fantastic, little one, he called you. He said he wanted to say hi. He's busy today and tomorrow too.

He asked me if I was leaving. He's teasing me. I tell him I want to see him today to give him his present and he, with that raking voice, "I know, but don't worry, I won't let you get away!" And then some banter about the country house, if I've decided what to do with it, a hotel or maybe a casino and he laughs, a false laugh.

He never calls me by name, never says his own. I didn't recognize him right away. "Oh! Alessandro." And he, "So many guys call you! I'm Marco." What a stupid idiot.

I don't know what's happening. I feel upset.

Medusa sees the Guardians of the Mountain

Ahead the guardians, the beasts. They are immobile yet they move incessantly.

Proud and vigilant she is at his left, beside the open sea. He is lying lightly on his right side, his body stretched out and his head held high and gently leaning toward her.

They are lovers not in love.

She is more lissome, protective. She inhabits her place calmly. He too is protective but more fully abandoned. He grants his undefended belly to the foam of the sea.

Huge monsters, tender and hot beneath a perennial sun, with water beating their flanks.

They love each other without needing to show it.

The lovers are recognizable only from behind. From the front they are nothing more than two stones split down the middle.

December 23

A sign. I need it. I don't want anything added to my fate.

My secret. Tomorrow I'll take care of my body. Renewed, I'll go to see the girls.

I won't wait for you. Yesterday you said hello as if you were running away: "See you later."

I'm still blowing bubbles. They dissolve like everything I know and forget. My waking up as a baby, or as the other one who's dying. The secret, yes, the sea the wood, the wood the sea.

Christmas Eve. The gloomy certainty of what no longer is. I wait. I'm still waiting for you to call and I've given you little time.

Dinner time. If you don't call then it means that it's too much. The lamp is over there, alone by now, today I was supposed to give it to you.

You'll get it later anyway but it won't be the same.

I'm not sad. I'm not and that's that.

And it starts up again and people use themselves up all on their own. An enormous waste, everything happens only inside me.

All right. So learn to wait well.

Almost four o'clock. Time was up at four.

Please.

Five minutes to four. Shitshitshit man why don't you love me.

It's four o'clock. Anyway who's going anywhere.

Big deal, staying home until the last minute so that if he calls I'll be here. I'd go to my parents' house anyway and meet up with him later.

A quarter past four.

Time passes, doesn't pass, I don't know.

The sun's gone down.

In the meantime I clean up. I read and throw away

papers, articles. What else can I throw away?

Myself, music and my notebook. A nice trio.

You've always loved three, right?

The music is awful and feels bad, like me.

I'm not desperate. I'm not and that's that.

Midnight by now.

I had to leave. At home, everybody, the Christmas tree and the presents.

The girls excited and happy. But I don't play with them, I pretend. I'm not into it and they know it, they leave me alone, I'm afraid.

I'm sitting next to papà on the couch. I've leaned my head on his chest and he puts an arm around my shoulders, hugs me.

"Papà," I said, "papà, I'm old." He looked at me and then asked me softly why I was talking like that. "I have so much past." His hand moves to my head, tousles me. "We all have a past." "But mine is too different." "It's because you haven't stopped yet," he said. And I think I won't stop. Papà is worried, he tries not to let it show. I'm a fool.

I feel his warmth and hear the happy voices, down below, coming from the kitchen. I'm still here, yes, and so is my old family. Who was saying that only the beginning and the end count.

The girls show up, beg me to stay after dinner so we can play cards together and then they run away. Papà hugged me harder, my grandmother's ghost at once overshadowed us.

Nonna at Christmas. In the kitchen, the realm of my mother becomes hers once more.

She with her big white handkerchief on her head and that smile handed out tasks to everyone. The party started with her. We already knew what would happen, it was like the feeling you get when you listen to the same fairy tale over and over. And she was so beautiful, afterwards, all dressed up.

The presents and finally the game. You loved to play cards but you never said so. We all smiled as we watched you and waited for the moment. It was papà who would say, "nonna, why don't you go get the money so we can play?" And she, with a twinkle in her eye, would act coy, "Not me, I'm old." Then we would wait for her to come back with a little purse that was always new in her hands.

Complicity, I want my people. I want to laugh together.

Where have my people gone?

Nonna, not even you exist any more.

Separations and abortions, shit.

I'm a little drunk, not totally.

It's better to go home. What am I doing here, at night, driving around in a parked car, writing.

I'd like to lose myself tonight and drink until I vomit and get myself all dirty, on the ground.

December 25

It's Christmas.

But the bells are beautiful.

Outside my sister's door I wait for them to return from mass. Tonight in the churches I look for silences.

I must seem a little crazy and strung out, they all look at me the same way.

A desire to laugh. Projects, today the wait will end.

If you don't come my life will go somewhere else.

It's four o'clock.

Run home and that unknown force that commands me.

You knew I was out for dinner today. It's Christmas, the present was for today. If you don't call me now it's over. Which would be better anyway.

Ridiculous. That present, there on the table, is ridiculous. If I give it to you I'll feel ridiculous.

He called, it's a quarter past four.

I don't know how I feel. "So! I got you."

It means he tried other times.

It doesn't matter, I'm tired.

Eaten up. Life's funny, especially me.

I think I want to cry. It doesn't come. Stiff and disappointed. Almost don't want to go. It will be the last night. I'm tired of this game. Life's funny, and yet you called in time.

I'm not happy even now.

Alessandro I'm telling you a story.

I'm sad. I woke up old today. My eyes that terrify, they look within and behind. Ahead there's nothing.

The real children, they never stop being children, they're children and that's that. Have you seen how great they are when they play, they pretend without needing to kill.

I with my ridiculous gift that I don't know how to throw away, it turns into a missed game. A missed dream. A whole bunch of pain is left that doesn't even hurt. It's nothing. Absolutely nothing.

The room watches me. It doesn't miss a thing.

Heavy, on this bed with the red quilt from when I was little. Even the smell is the same, my first room already full of phantasms.

Did you ever happen to think of yourself as if you'd never been born, or never died. It's all the same.

Today, stay like this for infinity.

Let everything run off your back. No, it's not water, it's heavy, like weariness. It drags you along the ground, it makes you want cool grass, the just-born, soft green that caresses your face when you lie down in it. Lying still in it with open hands, lying still you listen to its smell and you can even cry.

I'm not getting up anymore. I think I'll never get up again. I've arrived, arrived.

My hands need to move, I open them, I close them.

The pause always comes to an end and the smell of grass always vanishes.

Maybe the wind, or the end of the cassette. Yes, I still want to hear music, another one.

I look at your eyes.

The need to love. Why not.

When I used to get up while it was still dark out and go to the tree on the hill to watch the sun come up, I and the tree, patiently, keeping our gaze fixed on the depth that slowly was growing completely light. The tree was alone. Maybe that's why I loved it so much. Who knows what kind of tree it was, how it had come to be alone.

The river was shimmering. After I ran there. It was forbidden. The little beaches were dangerous. They seemed solid but you could sink down in them.

The adventure books I devoured at night made me keep going ahead like my Indians. A strange little girl. She was always living what she wasn't. So one day I ended up in an abandoned little shed full of shit that had looked solid. Cow dung always does that. I sunk right in with my bicycle, fell down, lost my shoes. Mamma slapped me, but I didn't care. It's just that I was ashamed. My quicksands.

The ridiculous.

My inadequacy was already with me.

The impossibility of my dreams, maybe I've always known it.

I have to go.

Fifth Day

His house, December 25, 1984

He's there in the kitchenette. She's looking around in the living room. She's uneasy. There's another arrangement now, even the bed has been moved away from the wall.

Fear, as subtle and heavy as fog, begins to rise up her legs. He's cleaning spots off the floor with a rag.

She takes in the penetrating smell spreading through the air as a reminder of the past. She was a small child. Their first move. The happy little girl ran around among the dismantled furniture. He, "Ammonia is the best thing for cleaning, and it costs less." They told her time and again to get out from under their feet but she loved to scamper between the basins and colored rags. She loved washing.

"Smell that stuff and see if it's still good." She remembers once again how very carefully she had carried out her task. Then fire from the water and she, wide-eyed, had followed it to the very last vapor. And then the darkness, her groping mouth and hands. And the laughter, "How can you be so stupid."

Standing up again she states, "So you're leaving."

He – "I'm really not sure yet. My friend . . . "

She – "I thought you were going alone."

He – "No, I was supposed to go with friend, but her boyfriend broke his leg and so we don't know yet."

She, sitting on the bed, wonders why he's reassuring her.

They watch TV in silence. She, curled up on the bed, thinks she should go to get the package she had left hidden on the easy chair but she can't manage to move. Her enormous, still eyes seem to be held together by a steel thread.

He gets up, takes a plastic envelope and without looking at it throws it on the bed in front of her. "Here, this is for you."

She rises, smiles. She sees herself take the envelope. She sees herself listen to its sound in her hands like crazed fountain pens scratching. There's still room, she patiently awaits the end of the sound. Two records and at the bottom a tiny little doll. "How cute, thanks." Now she's the one who gets up. She comes back with a package in her hand, sets it in front of him as he lies on his belly waiting.

Coldly she observes his hands and the changes in his face the entire time. She enjoys a useless victory.

He – "Ah, it's a lamp." He unwraps it more hurriedly. Then a silence and a whisper, "But how much did you pay for this." He takes the card and reads it with his back turned. She can barely see his profile. Her eyes, already drowned, follow his comments, "So, a multipurpose lamp. Yes, to tell the truth I could really use this."

Finally he laughs, she thinks, at the phrase "left over from the previous gift."

She – "Do you know hopscotch?"

He – "No. What is it?"

She – "It's the title of a book, but it's also a game children play. It has a lot of different names, where I come from we call it the bell game, the one with the stone in the squares, with one foot only, for reaching heaven. Haven't you ever played it?

He – "No." He gets up, puts the card back in the box.

He, with satisfaction in his voice, "This Christmas I got two useful presents. Another friend of mine gave me this steak cooker." He shows it to her. Meanwhile he moves around the room. He puts the cardboard box down again, arranges the lamp behind the bed, looks at it, says over and over, "I really like it, yes, I really like it." Without stopping, he looks for and takes down a large book full of photographs of remote Asian locations. "This is what I gave myself." He thumbs through it, tells her about it. He talks about the places he's already seen. He gets up, fishes around in a drawer, takes out small objects, souvenirs of his trips, shows them to her, asks her if she likes them, puts them in the plastic envelope. "I always bring a lot of them with me, I like to give them to the kids in my hometown." He stretches out on the bed, his impudent gaze fixes on her. "But you haven't really seen anything. What are you waiting for, sell the country house and go see the world, you can always find a real man along the way and maybe even make a kid, you just tie him on your back and take him along with you." That mocking voice upsets her, makes her incapable of doing anything. He continues, "Instead of coming down this alley you could take in the sunsets wearing a big cloak and maybe smoking opium, now that would make sense."

She remains silent, looks at the images running across the screen. A great dejection has invaded her, she tries to fight it off.

He, with changed voice, "Are you hungry? Do you want to eat?"

She – "No thanks, I've eaten so much today."

He – "Right, Christmas dinner. You said you went to your sister's. Tell me about your family."

She looks at him. "I wouldn't know where to start."

He – "Your father, what's he like?"

She smiles. "Papà is someone who knows what's what."

He – "So you have an enlightened father. And what does he say about life."

She, with faraway, shining eyes – "He says it's simple, you just have to know what you want."

He – "And what does he have to say about you?"

She – "He observes me."

He – "But what does he say."

She – "He's worried, but he tries to understand."

He – "O.K., but what does he say."

She – "He doesn't say anything, but he's there for me."

He – "And your mother?"

She lowers her eyes then looks at him, "Mamma is the other half of the sky."

He – "Then you're lucky. Do you see them often?"

She – "No, they don't live in Rome. They live in the country."

He – "In the country house?"

She – "No, but not far from there. And what about your parents?"

He – "My mother is dead and my father moves around."

She – "Don't you see him."

He – "Almost never."

She – "Don't you have a good relationship with him?"

He – "We don't have anything to say to each other." He gets up, finds a pack of cigarettes. "So if I came with you to your country house I could meet him?" His eyes deride her. "Or don't you let him meet your men. Tell me, come on, did he ever meet Gianni?"

She is looking for her tobacco, doesn't answer. A silence, then his voice, calmly, "What does your father say about people like us who don't know what they want?"

She – "He doesn't believe it." She slowly licks her cigarette, lights it and falls back across the bed.

He is still standing. "I have never known where I was going."

She turns her eyes toward him. "Maybe it's just a matter of having courage."

He – "Or doubts."

She – "Often it's just confusion. When I went to Delphi and saw the charioteer, I understood the difference.

I thought about all those people who sometimes had spent months waiting to get into the temple. They had traveled for months just to get there and never even asked about their future, just for help in resolving some doubt." She is all cuddled up, holding to her stomach a pillow she's pulled out from among the quilts. Taken by her own thoughts, she continues: "It's a question of desire. There's something that's more important than anything else, a center . . . "

He's sitting at the foot of the bed watching her, amused: "I like too many things."

She, serious, "Me too, but I mean that there's something that's absolutely true . . . "

He interrupts her, "So you're looking for unity, a lot of people have tried that and failed." He looks at her seriously, then, in a louder voice: "My grandmother was a gypsy and we say that an object loses its essence if you desire it too intensely."

He moves between rooms. "I have to bring the bike in, tell me if you're staying, otherwise I'll walk you to your car."

She – "What do you think?"

He – "Whatever you decide is O.K. with me."

She smiles in spite of herself. "O.K., I want to know what you'd prefer." He's in the other room, doesn't answer.

Her voice once again, loud, "What do you think about me staying?"

He's opening the front door. "You know I like it if you stay. If you want I can put it in writing."

A brief absence. In the meantime, she has begun to thumb through the book.

Already at the threshold he calls to her: "So when you sell the country house, you'll finally be living!"

She – "You really want me to go. What does it matter to you."

He – "Nothing. I could introduce you to the 'elite.'" He draws closer to her, his eyes impudent. "I saw Gianni a few days ago."

She – "Oh really?"

He – "We talked about you."

She – "No kidding!"

He – "Yes. He says terrible things."

She – "Like what?"

He – "Like you're a sex maniac."

She – "Really."

He – "Yes. He also says you're cuntocentric."

She – "What does that mean?"

He – "Phallocentric, cuntocentric."

She smiles. He starts to get ready for bed. She, in the bathroom, decides to talk to him. She prepares herself, as with a poem she's memorized.

They're in bed with the lights out. The lamp behind the bed doesn't work yet, there's no plug.

They barely hold each other, she's forgotten how her speech begins.

"Every time I come here it seems I have tasks to do, like tests. It's like a ritual."

He – "You honor me."

She – "I can't seem to stop it."

He – "Why not?"

She – "I don't know, maybe you're too strong for me."

He – "We knew that right from the start."

She doesn't answer. Time passes in silence. Suddenly she asks him, in a soft voice, "Have you never been in love?"

He – "Very seldom." He turns the other way.

She has a hard time sleeping. Lying awake, she dreams about his telling her "I've never kissed like you, with my mouth open."

They wake up together, their bodies draw close, they begin to touch each other. Then she stops. She doesn't want to keep on alone.

They remain very still. Then his loud voice: "Good morning! Slept well?"

She – "Well..."

He – "What did you dream about."

She – "I dreamt about this room, more or less as it really is."

He – "You have a great imagination."

She – "And what did you dream about."

He – "A revealing dream. Yes. I dreamt about a big house in the middle of a wood. I was watching from the road when all of a sudden I saw a dark form appear far off and come rushing toward the house. It was a bicycle with a man on it stubbornly pedaling along. The bicycle rider went past the gate and stopped under the trees next to a car. A man leaning out of the car's open window seemed to be waiting for him. It was your father."

She laughs quietly so as not to be heard. She pretends to be angry, says "give me a break" in a little girl's voice and turns the other way. She hopes he's laughing, she hopes his arm will keep her held to his chest.

He doesn't move. Flat on his back, with his arm beneath his head, he's lost in his own thoughts.

She abandons the game, turns slowly toward him, looks

at him, the room is still deep in shadow, she asks, "What are your dreams usually like?"

He – "Strange images. I'm there, I turn around and there are others, other me's . . . everyone is me." He kisses her on her forehead and says he has to get up, he has to meet someone.

They've just left Giolitti's. The sun is starting to feel hot and the air is like holiday air, you can see it and touch it, and the bells chase each other all over.

Together they head toward the Tiber, he is walking her to her car before he takes off.

While they're walking he talks about what he sees. His voice, sent forth and then taken back, always strikes the same points.

He – "Good guys are out of fashion, someone should hurry up and tell all the mothers."

She doesn't answer. She sees herself holding the arm of his leather jacket, listening. She thinks how her rage always turns to pain, compassion, almost never to hatred.

He sees a Great Dane go by. "You know, a friend of mine has a puppy, he wants me to take it. What do you think, is this as beautiful as the other one?"

She – "Yes, it's very beautiful."

Leaning against the parapet above the river they watch the water silently.

She is very tired, closes her eyes, would like to collapse be carried off.

He asks, "What are you going to do now?"

She – "I don't know. Ever since we talked about the country house I've had the urge to go there."

He – "Will you stay there until New Year's?"

She – "No, if I go, I'll go just for a day."

They stand next to each other in silence. Then, suddenly, he starts to kiss her tenderly on the cheek over and over again and without looking at her whispers, "I'll call you before New Year's."

She stands still, listens to her desire to go down the little stairs and get to the water. She turns. He's already crossed the street, he's far away. He looks at her, too, but pretends not to have done so.

She walks toward the stairs.

EXCERPTS FROM HER WRITINGS

December 26

The bells on the river, the harvest.
Now I want to get some sun.

The running water. Fear, the old fear.

There's wind, too.

My body all stretched out doesn't stay still, the cement is too cold and dirty. I'm afraid of rats.

Sitting still I wait for movement, it will expand.

My undone heart. I don't feel well, I didn't sleep last night.

Here I am trying to guess my life.

I don't know anything.

I don't know who you are.

Lost. I had to understand, decide during these months, instead they just went by, nothing.

Maybe I know the life I want. Like you say, a man, even one traveling around in the world, and a baby strapped on in front or in back, it doesn't matter.

Time is my enemy.

I'm still afraid of any old dog that comes down the stairs behind me.

My shoulders contracted.

Once you asked me what was the very first thing I would teach a child. "To laugh," I said. And you answered, "I'd teach him to watch out for his back."

Time is my enemy.

Cover my back. A secret to keep or to invent. But even secrets need light, just like dew.

To resist, nurture the seed distilled by white knuckles.

Time is my enemy.

I remember when my heart used to sing early in the morning, "I'll have lots of children and adopt some too . . . there's no limit, you can always carry them on your back."

A dream I missed out on.

Once the little girl, she was already big, said to me with a whining voice: "Dogs yes, but kids, no."

Time is my enemy.

I don't want to tell you my life story.

Everybody gets the children they deserve. I have rocked this love for you like a dead baby.

December 27

Find yourself again, lose yourself. Rhythms.

December 28

I listen to the music you gave me. I can't stand it now.

December 29

You don't understand, the past is dead, I am ready. You don't understand. I'm so cold, I don't want to get sick, but I feel something is slipping away. I can't hold things together any more. It's like the wax on this candle.

Today I got back to my papers, Medusa is waiting for me. But I don't have the courage to begin.

I have to lie down and stay that way. The ants advance in infinite numbers, they fall off the wall like newborn rats.

There is a time to fight and a time to die.

I lack courage.

Today I danced for you. With shackles on my ankles and my wrists tied together, I danced for you.

But you are far from what you know.

Today I was wandering around the house and I wanted you to be here, just this once. I wanted you to see.

I took all the old books from the shelves again, the

ones I read as a little girl. I went to get them from my parents' basement some time ago. The trunk like a precious jewel casket. There were no rats.

I brought them all with me. They smell like mold, damp. I like that. They look beautiful spread out on the ground on the red carpet, and sitting among them I see them in the mirror. I smile and touch my wrinkles, I smile at the affectionate voice telling me, "So, you're beginning to look like an old Indian chief."

I loved the Indians, I loved their silence and the immense space it contained. I loved the pride in their gazes, their strong, limber bodies. I loved them when they knelt down and bent their heads to the ground to pick up the echo of galloping horses.

I loved tracks the way I later loved scars. Now wrinkles are more difficult.

I laugh in the face of my fear, but, crouched, it lies in wait.

The Indians knew how to wait and their preparations for waiting filled me with admiration.

You've never even seen me.

"I condemn you to live in other forms in the den of the serpent and to return to earth each night to run a hundred times around the cemetery that holds your victim's remains . . ."

The spell. He ran so fast no one could see him. My favorite fable.

And you talk to me about complicity. More beautiful than love you said. Yes, and you know why? It takes two. You can die of love all alone.

You and your beautiful words, you drool them on yourself and run to wash them off.

In bed. It's very late. I have a high fever.

I don't like myself, everything's floating, I can't manage to find a still place, I don't like myself.

I need silence.

I'm not capable of praying.

I need help, give me anything and the humility to receive it.

. . . All those little white beds in a row and the children. The little girl is so pale. Leaning over her I caress her forehead. My little one, you've been here so long. We just about gave up on you.

But today is a holiday, we're going out in a while, they're coming to get us. Your mother can't stay still, her little girl is coming home, she's there now getting ready for your arrival.

My soul, now I can look at you without dying. How pale you are.

Bent over her I hear it come. She writhes, shakes her head harder and harder. "Take it easy, little one, it's nothing it will be over in a minute I'm here with you."

And then she, her eyes closed so that she barely peeks out, lifted her little hand, searching, found my lips and then traveled down slowly onto my breasts and was stammering unconnected words about a teddy bear finding its den.

My soul, now I can look at you without dying. I feel you rustling around in my chest.

I stay whole inside your closed eyes.

December 30

Today is a good time for throwing stones.

Four. At the fourth space I always make a mistake. The stone goes out-of-bounds or stops.

December 31

And today a good time to die.

Medusa is still waiting on the rock. This morning I got up wanting to work. He has certainly left. I have to be sure.

I want a good ending. That's all I can do. Outside I hear the New Year's celebration. The last day of the year.

I thumb through my work. The syntheses slip past me. The syntheses, a danger, eat life up. Only a few of them pry open doors, a flash strikes and that's it.

"Passion, an art fallen into disuse." The title of a pamphlet for a sculptor's exhibition. I still remember him finishing his work all white with powder and a hat made from a newspaper on his head, he looked like a stone mason.

Then I laughed.

Here's the New Year

Swollen and wet.

Curled up on the bed as if I were in the womb, my hand moves my soul from behind, that little one down there comes out only slowly, sometimes coaxed, licked, cuddled. Too many years, too much living with losses inside, inside a hand a tongue a body, two dismembered eyes together inside, yours mine theirs I don't know, everyone's.

O.K. I raise my hand and drink to you who have left.

I give you Medusa.

MEDUSA

Past the Ocean, at the world's westernmost point, lives Medusa, the Queen.

Reaching her realm is an arduous task. The road is long, and few know the way. If you ask them, not even the youngest goddesses can tell you how to get there, perhaps not even Athena.

The dominion of the night reaches deep into forests that grow ever thicker, ever more menacing with cold. Like thunder locked in the earth, the wind promises an eternity of sudden storms. Here and there, as if dropped from uneven rainfalls, shining rocks bloom like roses.

The land of rock roses is its other name.

Suddenly in view, a strip of land rises like an angry serpent's neck toward the sky.

Stretching into emptiness, it stands like a lopped-off tongue. A motionless point heavy with silence at the borders of life where night blends into day.

A curling chaos of rocks marks its boundaries. Behind it lies the harsh access route. In front, a lone white road wends sharply down to the great rock rose lying at the edge, an embroidery darkening the rim of the abyss.

Boundless as a desert, the sea spreads out below, blurs into the sky and falls silent.

Sun and moon never grace this shade. And light captured by the darkness imprisons your eyes like an echo.

Among these sullen, savage shapes you can make out the entry to the caves. All in a line, they look like nests impatient beaks have carved.

From one of these holes Medusa emerges.

She straightens up and stands quietly on the threshold. Huge, her ink-dark eyes pale in her ashen face, and her black garment gathers the silence of her concealed body.

Her gaze moves among the shadows like a slow caress. With the last fire gone only stone remains. She listens to its sounds, one by one.

Never has she found it so lovely.

Her greeting finished, she places her still unbelieving fingers upon her crystal-smooth head, so lovely. It almost seems she's smiling. Then she lowers her hands, folds them, and begins her evening walk, slow upon the white road.

Having climbed to her spot between the folds of the rock, she curls up her young body. For a long time she remains crouched on her knees, her hands open, loose, and her eyes immersed far away.

Now and then her distant face seems to awaken. An impossible torment lights it up and then suddenly leaves it like wind dying down. The final rebellion. Then a new pride raises her to her knees, and her lips part.

"Hear me, Athena, hear me. I am ready.

Now I can speak. I wish yet to hear my own voice, out loud, for song is permitted before dying.

Next to my cot I found my new dress and the lifeless snakes. Futile joy ran through me quicker than lightning. I have never begged for your forgiveness. I do not repent.

I accept as a final gift my ancient form and my heart, swollen like a sponge in water. I know what they cost.

I have gone down into the abyss you gave me. Emptied, I forgot my body so completely that I almost stopped breathing.

Faith was my sun.

I heard noises lurking in the deep silence, and I followed them until I no longer knew where I was.

I delighted in the enchantment of sounds and the names of things.

I sacrificed my voice to imitate the secret music until I had broken all the voices. The echo of my screams lit up the pathway, and hunger made it clear.

Time came over me.

I touched the heat of the hawk's new-born feathers and the snake's dry skin, as fragile as paper aged in the sun.

In absolute silence I heard the rocks grow. I heard them speak. Their rumble was like thunder lit by lightning in spring. I heard them roll around between the feet of secret dancers like stars in the sky. And I, too, danced all the worlds together.

I let the fire burn me.

And the sea's perfume.

I understood the tree, and its sky-bound roots.

My rebellion spent, I laughed with excitement and heard the song of the broken heart.

Listen to me. I believed until I and faith became one.

Listen to me. The horizon which once held my gaze is no longer enough.

This sea is but a lake.

The sky is no more, and the light, below, is only pretending.

My rock is but a place to sit.

Yes, I am ready."

The Light One and The Dark One look into each other's eyes.

Medusa stays where she is, turning only her gaze toward the right. Athena, at the foot of the rock, is almost even with her height.

M. – Now I can look into your eyes. I have accepted my fate.

A. – Your fate was already sealed.

M. – My questions press for answers.

A. – You disobeyed.

M. – I merely loved.

A. – Your heart was too hot, and you dreamed the impossible.

M – I fail to understand what guilt there is in that.

A. – It is not yours to understand but to accept, as all mortals must.

M. – You, the maiden warrior, have condemned me. Tell me the truth.

A. – You wanted to be a goddess.

M. – You held back my life.

A. – I had no choice.

M. – You let me think it possible.

A. – You could have done it only as a slave. The choice mortals must make does not spare useless courage.

M. – You surely wouldn't know. You, the virgin warrior who spurns men's seed, the clear-seeing one, the just one, the keeper of all sad secrets. You have a kingdom to maintain.

The desecrated temple still bears the color of your dress, the ice of your clear blue eyes.

You stood in my way, you kept me from the underworld that leads to life.

A. – The underworld is the pain of those who do not love. It does not belong to woman.

M. – In a man I would have wished for all my soul has ever desired.

A. – You have known other things, and your eyes retain those memories. Their color was distilled from your solitude. Bodiless, you shall continue to be queen of your realm. A horrible presence there on the threshold, you will be the one to bar the way. They will respect you and eat upon your body forever.

M. – No one will rescue me.

A. – Even heroes will tremble at the thought of meeting you.

M. – Just like the heart of one who loves, you, too, need secrets. Tell me the truth. Why such a long wait? What do you want from me?

A. – I want the color of your eyes. On my breast.

They fall silent.

A. – The time has come. The boy is about to arrive.

M. – I'll wait for him here.

Her eyes drift far off once again.

M. – I have one request. Have him wait a while so I can see one more time.

Light up this sky. Make the night shine so the moon may devour me like a sun burning out. And like the stars when they draw rainbow arcs like arrows from a bow and then grow dark. I want to see this sluggish water shattered by the wind so that huge foam-swollen waves will rise high and crash back down. And the ship tossed by the waves below.

I want to see the morning and its dew shine on this black earth.

By now Athena is far away. Her voice carries back, "Look, the moon is already high."

Telling stories about what an easy task he's been given, Perseus laughs and, never one to miss an opportunity, adds, "Women! They make so much out of nothing."

EPILOGUE

Rome, April 30, 1985

My work is finished. The last meeting today at her house.

I hadn't seen her for quite awhile. Before she left we agreed to use the last day of the year as the end of the story. All the rest a useless repetition. She took on the task of making up a file about the "after."

Today our last meeting.

I found everything ready, as usual. On the coffee table there was even dessert and a bottle of good wine. "To celebrate," she said.

I got ready. Today I didn't need the tape recorder. I let my gaze roam. A different room looked back at me. No longer the cheerful disorder that had accompanied us on our journey. The soft pillows scattered and tangled with the comforters on the floor are now all lined up, stiff and a bit sad, as if they were waiting. The desk is empty and the papers that used to be strewn everywhere have ended up packed inside the folder, which is too small, and tightly bound with long colored ribbons. I remember the day we began, when she had such a good time showing me her creation—will we ever manage to complete it?—she would ask me doubtfully each time we felt we were incapable of following our pathway. A big envelope with "For You" written on it attracts my attention. I look at it, curious and amused. She always has some surprises for me.

The smell of coffee, and she arrived right away. She looks well but she's lost a lot of weight.

When she was sitting across from me, her place, we

looked at each other. The end of our voyage.

She – "What made you think of decaf?"

I – "Decaf?"

She laughed. "You'll see."

I – "How did the seminar go?"

She – "Interesting."

Her eyes turn away. I've learned to respect her silences.

She – "I conquered the four. I had an abortion."

In that very moment I realized that my eyes were fixed on the beautiful red velvet rose, a little worn but illuminated like old paintings. I wondered how I had failed to notice it before.

Then I asked if it was from him.

She – "No. I would have kept it. One night I made love with a friend. Wanting to be loved a little, wanting to have my body back. Seventh day of my period, being careful, and also you know only half of me works. I got pregnant. It didn't make sense.

"When the doctor asked me during the exam if I had had other abortions, I felt ashamed, I felt desperate to justify myself. So I told him how it had happened. He listened to me carefully and then began to nod his head. He said he believed me even if women usually tell endless lies, his words." Instantly her smile flares up. "Recent studies of reliable American researchers have noted the capacity of some women to provoke ovulation during sexual relations, as do rabbits," he said. "These are only simple hypotheses, still unproven, but they must make us think."

She – "I couldn't do anything else. If I love a man, only a baby with him is possible. I couldn't do anything else. What kind of a world is this, where love produces death?"

She looked out the window. "I've come back. I feel alive. I cleaned the whole house and found Rome in springtime again. Don't you smell its perfume?"

I – "When did it happen?"

She – "A few days ago. I went somewhere else for everything, had the best possible conditions, was with another woman." She looked at me, "Well, it's the same old solution once more."

I – "You'll see him again."

She – "I don't know. You should ask me if I'm going to avoid him. I don't know. During these past months I haven't managed to free myself from him, in fact, not even my work has let me do that, no, it hasn't. That's why I'm glad this is the last day." She gets up slowly, takes the envelope labeled "For You" and hands it to me with a faint smile. "Inside this you'll find my final entries, the short notes on my last meetings with Alessandro, and the letter I wrote to you from the hospital. As you see, you were there with me." Her eyes wander away again and remain distant.

But I have one remaining doubt. A doubt I need to resolve on my own. Shall we begin?"

FROM HER FILE (JANUARY 4 – 24, 1985)

Friday, January 4

He calls. Stupid jokes right off the bat, his voice exasperating. "I thought you'd gone," I said. A dry no for an answer. He'll call next week seeing as how I have the flu and he doesn't want to catch it.

Monday, January 7

Unexpectedly in the morning his beautiful voice on the phone. Snow last night. He tells me about frozen pipes and a broken water heater. He might need some help to go buy a new one. Yes, I'm available, my car's working.

Later he calls me. Everything's solved. He'll be in touch.

Wednesday, January 9

He tells how he's balancing on rooftops. He spends his time unfreezing pipes. He asks me if I'm coming out this afternoon, but I can't. I'm waiting for the doctor. He teases me. "Why don't you come over here?" He says he can't, he has to take care of the gas canister, it's run out, he has to get a new one. Maybe he can get over tonight. I waited in vain without believing him too much.

Thursday, January 10

Evening. His voice just to tell me he'll call tomorrow. "I waited for you yesterday." "I know," he said. "I couldn't come. I'm totally taken up by the house."

Friday, January 11

His voice asks if my car is still working. He contrives laughter. If I go over there he can load all his dirty clothes into my car and take them to the laundry. I can't and I don't want to. I don't feel well. I manage to ask, "But what about you, do you want to see me, car or no car?" "Yes, of course," he answers. "I have some practical problems to solve."

I announce my possible availability for the next day. He'll let me know.

Sunday, January 13

Saturday he didn't call. Sunday, upset, I decide to go over to his place.

It's almost evening. I climb the stairs. I knock. His voice comes asking at the door. I say my name. In the silence I look at the door that opens but not all the way. He slides out through the crack.

I look at him without seeing him. "Hi, am I bothering you?" He says no but doesn't move. I ask if I can come in and he, "Actually I'm with this friend right now." I stammered something, some excuses, I think, and a goodbye. He stopped me, "Listen, we can get together later. Come back in two hours." I said no. No, it doesn't matter. And he asked me, "Where are you going now?" But I didn't know where I'd be going. And he, again, "If you go home I'll call you later." I think he was worried, but I really didn't know anything. "I don't know," I repeated. And then he raised his arms as if to say more than this he couldn't do. Then he threw me a little kiss with his hand. He closed the door.

Maybe he felt sorry for me.

The only thing I remember about that night was that I wandered around for a long time beneath the eaves full of already-old snow. There was water everywhere. The deafening noise finally calmed me down.

How much useless pain, my friend.

Later at home I even laughed. I saw his face saying the words "Actually I'm with . . . ."

Monday, January 14

The voice I love is calling me. "Where were you last night, I looked for you until it got late. Shall we get together?" I answered yes.

An appointment at ten o'clock tonight.

I climb his stairs again. I had sworn never again would I stop in front of that door. My first mistake, that night, betraying my promise. I thought I was wanted. He had looked for me, called me. But the golden scepter would not touch me. I knew it as soon as I saw him. The massacre started right away. Astonished, I saw my condemnation in his smile. We were in his room. His voice, his face, his gestures, everything was contorted and even violent.

" . . . Great. You've stopped being penned in at home waiting for the doctor . . . you don't know how to take risks . . . you can't make decisions . . . you have to see everything perfectly clearly first. I ask you to do me a favor and you want to know do I want to see you. You don't answer. One foot here and the other one there. Smart, attractive even, but down deep a little country girl who's read a few books."

He walks around the room, picks up a little book. He throws it on the bed next to me. Then he comes over and opens it. "While you were waiting for your doctor I went to a girlfriend's house and got this book for you. Read here, read it." Like an idiot with the open book in my hands, I read. It was the story of a meeting between a father and a son in the desert.

As soon as I raised my eyes he started in again. He moves from here to there and back again, fast and nervous. He picks up an object behind the partition, a cassette he practically throws into my hands, then he comes close. "I taped this for you." It had no cover, it was old and covered with erasures. Stretched in front of me he started to touch me as if he were pushing. I stayed still, motionless, nothing more. He kept on, he was taking my hand putting it on him and his mouth was pushing mine and all pressing and yelling, you know.

But I was watching it happen. I couldn't do anything else.

I don't know how much time passed. As usual, words remain like tangled anchors or stones thrown into the water of a raging river you have to cross. I don't know. What's left when there are no more things or when there never has been anything.

We were still lying across that bed our bodies had made hot. I felt heavy and empty like a can that's just been thrown out. I was in his arms, against his chest when he said, "You don't like me the way you used to. I'm sorry, for you, naturally. You haven't understood anything (pause) about life."

Then, slowly, he stretched his arms, his body, and said, "I want a decaf. You make me think about decaf."

Tuesday, January 15

He calls to find out if I like the cassette. For the first time, "A hug for you."

Friday, January 18

His goading voice and then, suddenly, a question that matters. He hangs up, "See you next week."

I had been reading a book he'd lent me. My task. As expert seer, I have steeped myself in the old putrefying water. He had disappeared. I read fast. Enough, I said, enough. I repeated this for a whole day as I walked around my house. I decided to go as one final test.

I saw the witches tied up in the water, life, the price of impossible innocence.

Thursday, January 24

He was sleeping. "I brought back your book." He says he'd forgotten about it. He asks me to come in, slips back under the quilt. I try to remember what I have to say. Already paralyzed I listen to his biting voice. I start to die. I try to move. "Alessandro, why can't I manage to break . . . " He interrupts almost violently: "If you're losing sleep over this you're crazy."

I'm speechless again. The goodbyes begin. I look around. The room is drowned in shadows and the objects suffocating together seem to be lying in wait. The wooden ceiling is beautiful, I look at it a long time as I lie on the bed. It reminds me of the country house.

He talks, all his voices, but I stop following them. I listen to the closed door. I take all the time I need. This is the ceremony of parting.

From the midst of the cut branches he drags in front of me I pluck only the coarsest one.

I – "If you like them so much why don't you go to the South Seas?"

He – "Because deep down this is my place. I'm a child of this time. And anyway I don't know how to swim. I don't like it. Once in Java I took a motorboat and went out to sea to jump off and see what would happen. Then I thought it was stupid, I didn't like it."

I'm done. I get up. He has to go out too, he says he'll come with me.

He offers me a book to read, I refuse.

Walking along arm in arm, but the rite is missing. The alley, the piazza and us inside the nighttime white. I know I will never forget.

Say goodbye.

Walk without hurrying like people who go home together. I felt his body on the wrong side. I don't know how to look to the right very easily. I felt his heat.

A quiet walk.

Conversation.

The finale.

He – " . . . And so they come over just in time for dinner, like they hadn't planned it. Does that ever happen to you?"

I – "No."

He – "You have thoughtful acquaintances."

I – "I don't have acquaintances."

He – "O.K., friends."

I – "If my friends are hungry they eat."

He looked at me ironically, "Our stories are really different."

He stops suddenly, "I'm going back, where are you headed?"

I answer with a gesture pointing to a little street on the left.

Silently he offers me his cheek, I turn mine to him, and almost without stopping we go our separate ways.

Before disappearing around the corner I heard his voice, loud, "We really made a U."

. . . Hospital, April 20, 1985

My friend,

I should tell you about the letter U but I can't. I'll do it when we speak.

In a few days we'll get together and it will all be over. How quickly you become the past, nostalgia.

Difficult days. I'm writing these last lines from the hospital.

In this empty, unadorned space, the whiteness of the walls and uniforms wounds my eyes. No consolation.

Sometimes I think that afterwards I'll realize I've become old.

The patina of time, heat, like the hidden speck of fire. I don't find it.

My eyes useless, I have braided and strung up rope bridges as in a dream. You can't escape the spell by yourself. From the start, I passed through all the doors, one after another. I couldn't get lost. Obligatory tracks, deep, I always fell in the same place.

I'm tired. I ask my executioner how much time is left . . . for everything.

Soon they'll come for me.

But I'm not alone. Marta and I came to the hospital yesterday. Our room has only two beds, a miracle. Our things are here and the camera is on the table. An extraordinary event brought us here together. Two friends sharing a bitter story. Gossip, silences, and hands that quickly clasp each other, it bewilders us.

We even laugh.

Eating soup with our hands. Did you know hospitals don't have silverware?

Hiding a broken glass from the disapproving nurse.

And we pushed the bed guards down right away, a hellish noise.

Now and then the muffled cries of newborn babies.

Time is my enemy.

I'd like to get up, I'm hungry. But I can't eat.

My lowered eyes gather in the sentence, "All or nothing."

And I'm here kneeling on the floor. I take up once again the work I've been assigned.

Precious drops as if distilled from rocks bathe me completely. May water shine burnt by the sun ever anew!

In the dark earth my hand follows clearer contours. The snagging stones, braided like antique carpets, release rays that flow everywhere. Rain of fire, invented pathways, panting like fireflies in the wheat fields at night. Golden threads that are finally sewn into young pools, stars, islands already prepared to die. And I watch, I watch, breathlessly.

Still the drops adorn me and roll down like river pearls.

Let the wetness remain, and also the odor of living things! When I've finished, I know, I'll see the whole design.

NOTES ON PERFORMING MEDUSA

The performance must give the impression of following a precise track.

These two quotations help me explain the meaning of this track.

1. That which has a beginning, a middle and an end is whole (Aristotle).

2. What we call the beginning is often the end. And to make an end is to make the beginning. The end is where we start from (T.S. Eliot).

The strength that comes from the first quotation should be the work's structure, along with the rhythm and tension generated by an inevitable and consciously chosen pathway, that of Medusa. The sacrifice must be complete and performed in the original sense of making oneself holy, as an act of creation (the only one possible).

The esoteric key to the text should in any case guide the performance.

In alchemy the fourth nature represents unity. The Pythagoreans stated that the four stood for the concretization of harmony in visible forms. It corresponds to the four directions of the universe and to the elements.

The marriage that leads to the birth of the hermaphrodite is symbolized by fire born out of water, the fourth nature, to be precise.

Thus Medusa represents the impossibility of marriage.

The passage Medusa completes should be subdivided into four parts:

1. Introduction
2. Medusa when she comes to the rock and speaks
3. Medusa and Athena

4. The completion of the sacrifice.

A very mobile, mute chorus should prepare the following actions and also function as a link to the whole. One could speak of phases that are constantly announced ahead of time and then executed.

The law of duality governs the movement of the entire performance which nonetheless is experienced as separation, lack of fusion and harmony: only the chorus moves. Medusa has a nonexistent body but a very strong, unadorned head and face. Medusa only speaks.

Athena, on the other hand, is perfect and whole in her total fiction (she could wear a costume).

The lack of equilibrium between the parts is expressed by a rhythm or energy that resembles a caterpillar's movements.

Thus the 4 is never complete. The work represents the impossibility of marriage either as a pathway belonging to the inside of each character or—and all the more so—between a man and a woman (the final scene).

The stone remains (one must look for the principle of life in that which is entirely without soul).

The final phase, the performance of the sacrifice, should come as a surprise and serve as a denouement.

When Athena and Medusa remain silent and Medusa says her prayer, the lights move onto a man and a woman who from the beginning of the performance have cut the scenic space along a diagonal by walking very slowly. The woman precedes the man and their almost imperceptible march maintains the same distance between the two of them until the lights come on her. She will be the one to perform the sacrifice. While the words of Medusa's prayer are being heard, the woman performs a brief dance (her movements come from T'ai-Chi-Chuan), the man joins her, she kneels, and without any interruption he continues on his walk with her head.

In practical terms we are concretizing the image in Rodin's sculpture.

The chorus will have rehearsed this scene, which continues in motion while the curtain closes.

The chorus must be entirely invented, as must the game of silences and music, spaces and directions.

The Eliot quotation explains what I would like the audience to feel at the end of the performance.

What comes to my mind are augury and even hope.

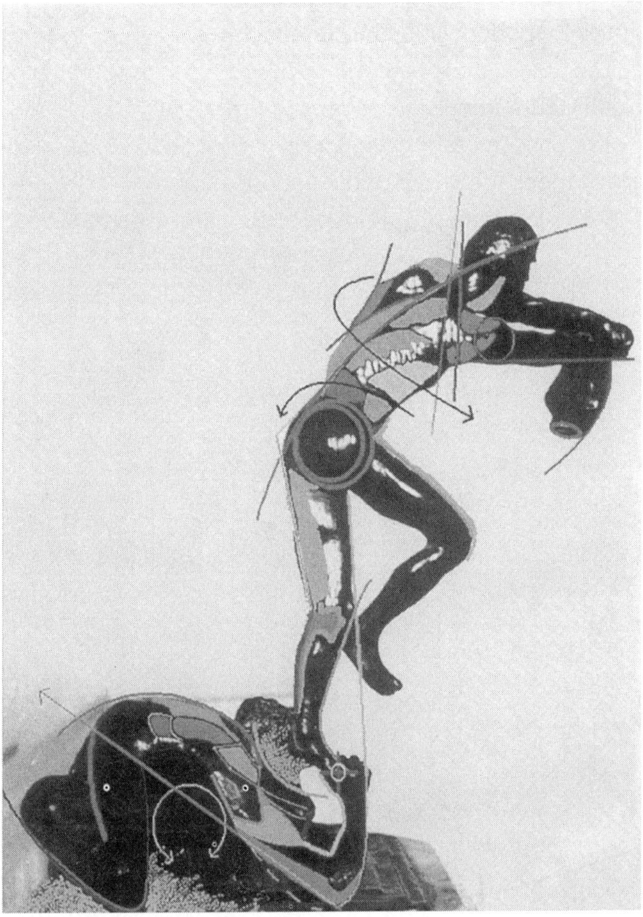

THE AUTHOR'S REFUSAL TO WRITE AN INTRODUCTION

Dear Editor,

I am sorry but I cannot write an introduction to *Medusa* that will clarify the hidden levels of the text, nor can I make more comprehensible the multiple threads of the characters' motivations and relationships. The fact is that the substance and essence and also the intention of *Medusa* is to touch something secret, intimate, and to bring it to light on several levels of reality.

It is difficult to explain this text because it tries to point toward and even to touch the nonreferential realm of the shadow (the *ombra*). In this dimension, the play of language allows for resonances, associations, analogies. Language creates images that then become subjects, somewhat like those Chinese boxes, one inside the other, each one smaller than the last—the well-known infinite regress or *mise-en-abîme*.

Because of this, it is difficult at times to pin things down. Thus the key word in describing what I want in my writing is "precision," not "clarity." The ambiguity of the Italian verb in relation to more than one possible grammatical subject is something for which I purposefully strove. Such ambiguity creates a middle ground where things cohabit and are not mutually exclusive. This is quite different from confusion. To try to approach this median "place," I have had, on the one hand, to deconstruct and dematerialize my signifiers and, on the other hand, to create a rigorous structure that gives the reader an Ariadne's thread to follow.

If I could sit down and chat with you, I would tell you all about my long period of preparation for writing *Medusa*, I would tell you about my research and the books that opened doors for me. Giordano Bruno's works are foremost among these, seeing as how we are speaking of shadow and also of magic. In *Medusa*, only an echo of my long preparatory work remains. Mine has been a precise choice, a choice I reaffirm today.

But then, if you were here in Rome, I'd ask you to meet me in Campo De' Fiori one evening. I suggest the evening because during the day the market invades the piazza and, among the colorful stands, the austere statue that reigns in the center of the square is overwhelmed by the cheerful movement of shoppers and sellers. Giordano Bruno was burned alive on February 17, 1600 on this very spot. At sunset, the dark, hooded figure (it's a bronze statue) that shows him standing with a book in his hands arrests the eye. I like to look at it as night falls, with the sound of running water (never absent in Rome) and the pigeons still as can be, perching on his shoulders like so many distracted guardians, shadows themselves of divine messengers, ancestors of the world.

While the light imperceptibly grows dim, I think about Bruno's work, and the "shadow-ness" at its heart. The substance of worlds—the possibility of grasping the unity of reality and the inner bonds that traverse it—nests between light and shadow. In that very nexus lies the foundation of knowledge of all things. Bruno speaks of a rich reality where planes and levels flow through each other without any hierarchies, where the only law is a constant exchange among all those that participate. The goal of wisdom is to discover the plot at work in the universe. To unveil its intrigues and infinite combinations, however, has a precise, operative meaning: to know and transform the world.

Consider the Philosopher-Magician who works with the Art of Memory, the furious sage bent on changing the inner universe. Here, always, the fullness of life with its limitless possibilities, triumphs.

But Bruno's extraordinary modernity, the modernity that condemned him to myth, has not become our own. Still needy and miserable today, we "moderns" flounder in a ridiculous binarism that excludes, that claims impossible certainties, that goes against us, breaks us in two and sentences us to shabby daydreams, shadows themselves of a lost creative imaginary, one that was mad, wise, courageous, and free.

My *Medusa* starts here, at this stupid imprisonment and aims to arrive elsewhere.

Monsters and demons inhabit the shadows. Who better than Medusa, the Gorgon par excellence, could guide my hope to "enter the inside." On the other side is the dreadful cry that enchants beings forever torn between attraction and horror. No one better than she represents extreme otherness in all possible forms. In ancient Greece the Gorgon's head inspired a holy dread. She is the Lady of the threshold that cannot be crossed, the monster who kills with her glance. But, above all, that head severed from the body represents absolute disorder. A disquieting combination abolishes categories generally kept separate. Its features annul the distinction between gods, humans, and beasts. She shows herself only from the front, and to see her means to measure yourself against her Power, a power of death that undoes all resistance and drags you into that dark world. It turns you to stone (the meanings of this symbol are infinite!), kills you. But petrification in many ancient initiation rites is a necessary stage so that ritual death may be accomplished and bring the initiate to a new birth.

To look Medusa in the eye seems to me an extraordinary opportunity, a magnificent undertaking. I felt ever more attracted to and fascinated by this idea. Only a woman could have the courage to accomplish it, I said to myself. So I began to draw close to her, slowly, yes, with love. A long journey. The main thing was to activate that plurality of planes and levels that infuse life with the stubborn hope of awakening. A kind of integral realism capable of taking into account both the daily nature and the magical aspects of reality and, even more, the soul's transformations. And then to wait, listen without resisting, and look.

To enter this realm, I have used two different languages or "persons." The technique of reconstruction let me use "the play of subjects" and an unusual "movement" of the narrative first person. Thanks to this way of narrating, I could use "partially" already extant categories, which I then abandoned with the precise aim of showing their partial nature. The third person narrates the "Day" encounters. The first person emerges as a result of excerpts from the diary of "Lei," [She] who is the protagonist of the novel, and functions something like La Maga in Cortázar's *Hopscotch*. The two languages alternate with mathematical precision, and represent two different kinds of subject, that is, two different ways of looking at reality. The fact that only at the end, in the Epilogue, these two voices take on bodily form, become two people, is the crucial innovation and originality of this book. This is the pillar of the work. The discovery at the end must be a surprise, a spur to reread the whole preceding book with different eyes. The alternation of subjects, with their different points of view, is the expression and the ambition of my way of writing, my poetics.

Closeness and distance determine the book's vision of

reality. This strategy arises from my long-standing interest in Max Planck. For me Planck's quantum physics is a key to reading realty. As the distance between the observer and the observed changes, the relationship between them changes. The closer the observer gets to the observed, the more heat there is. Nothing is stable here. (The heat is also the agent of effecting an alchemical transformation.)

Medusa is a "hot" book. One goes in very close and practically touches the cruxes, knots or matrices of consciousness and self-consciousness. (English has no equivalent for *coscienza*, which refers both to meaning and to how that meaning is constructed.) *Medusa*, therefore, works with emotions and catalyzes different identifications depending on the reader's own experience and level of development. (*Medusa* is the mirror of the reader and originates a myriad identifications.) Our task is to guarantee a faithful translation because the several levels of the text can appear only if there is a rigorous translation of the words. The words generate the hidden meanings, which cannot be explained with discursive clarity. One can only suggest, and then hope that the suggestions are picked up. Each reader will take away what he or she wants to and what he or she can.

In a book of this kind that has as its aim "the transformation of the reader," one cannot know everything from the start. On a journey one learns things by encountering them step by step. One must let oneself go. It is an initiation journey "to the feminine," in the water, in the waters. The deepest feelings, heated by passion, are the material and substance of the journey.

I'd also like to respond to another of your concerns about the characters. You see, in this novel they are all nothing more than shadows, exiles, some dense and others less so. They appear and disappear with no apparent reason. Only She, the nameless protagonist who has succeeded in refusing a role, finally achieves an identity, by her progressive identification with Medusa.

Alessandro, too, is a shadow. He represents an essence that I would define as the refusal to be. He is absent. He is afraid to begin. Thanks to Alessandro's refusal, She begins her research, her internal journey. It is important to run up against this "no" because only then does one begin to find out who one might be. Therefore, it is important not to specify Alessandro as if he were an empirical being. He does not actually take any particular action, and he does not open himself to being known in any particular way. (We do find out at the end that he has never confronted the Father and, therefore, authority.) He becomes an allegory of the situation of men today, of their immobility in an old, dead role that they, nevertheless, can't let go of.

The story of the two, She and Alessandro, is, in a certain way, the least important thing in the book. It is the exterior form of personal, solitary dramas. Each figure is alone, confined to her and his own story. Except for the Fourth Day, they never make deep contact. The difference between She and Alessandro is that he never moves, while she departs on a journey. The important thing is that she undertakes the journey to know herself and to be born as a complete subject, to attain unity. This is the "Alchemical Wedding," an initiation rite in which the subject must descend within herself, understand herself, and reach the third phase, that of freedom and love.

The point of departure is an "identification," or better, a recognition that permits her to measure herself against her own memories, incapacities, fantasies, and so forth. In this process, a parallel appears ever more clearly, a resemblance between Alessandro's incapacity and that of She's mother, a grievous incapacity to express and live love. The books Alessandro loans her are expressions, like those of her mother, of what he cannot express. There are many examples like this in the book, which is a tapestry of this kind of expression. They are there, one has only to stop and gather them. I really think that explaining does not help. We can give or take only what is already ours.

I hope that *Medusa* makes evident that woman cannot resolve her existence through romantic love, that such a relationship will not solve her problems. She will not get anywhere by projecting solutions onto the other person. This book declares that her journey exemplifies this necessity of first realizing herself as a subject. Only in this way will it be possible for her to free herself from the old roles (already dead anyway) that have governed relations between the sexes for millennia.

Finally, the numbers. The magic of the numbers is a game, an even lighter shadow than the others (mysticism as mathematics). In the ancient traditions of all peoples, the philosophy of numbers was cultivated and a rich system of symbols, of more or less secret correspondences, was generated, and it has marked our culture. In this book I employ multiples of four. For example, in the Pythagorean system the Four represents the concretization of the harmonies in visible form, the elements, the coordinates of the universe. In alchemy the fourth nature represents Unity, the symbol of which is the fire that is born from water.*

*The Four is not fully realized as I explain in the Notes on Performing *Medusa*, p. 178. The end notes direct readers to further references to these subjects.

The Fourth Kingdom is Medusa, this Medusa, condemned, who courageously dares to meet her executioner, Athena, in order to ask the question (the question is a bridge between two opposed orders, the essence of the exchange, of the relationship).

It is in the myth, in this meeting between Medusa and Athena (belly-head, emotion-reason), in the dialogue between the two figures, that an integration, always denied to the feminine (and not only to the feminine), is achieved. It is *the trace of a difference,* the beginning of a different possible future. Finally, a variant of the old myth. A kind of minor magic, certainly a shadow, dense and heavy, but daughter of memory and enchantment.

By the way, I received a warm letter about Medusa and thought I'd pass on this on to you: "Your book Medusa is not an erotic text, except in the sense that *all powerful books are.* And yours seems to be one of those."

One last thing, Medusa is also only a shadow. Don't cast too much light before you publish . . . .

I am sure that you will understand, and I thank you already.

Marina Minghelli
Roma, 1998

AUTHOR'S NOTES

p.3, line 1: M. Sosa is an Argentine singer. The song is "Soy pan, soy paz, soy mas," the line in the original text is "No quiero mas de lo que quieras dar" (I want no more of what you want to give).

p. 8, line 28: "If you know it I'll tell you, if you don't, I won't." *The Language of Madness*, D. Cooper

p. 24, line 19: "It is *Cassandra's* evening." *Cassandra*, C. Wolf

p. 25, line 1: "How can someone be loved very much? By being very powerful and not inspiring fear." *Parallel Lives: The Life of Alexander*, Plutarch

p.39, line 4 from bottom: "It's not indifference that steals weight from the image but love, extreme love." *Camera Lucida*, R. Barthes

p. 42, line 7: "And with her he lay in the soft field and midst the spring flowers." *Theogony*, Hesiod

p. 50, line 16: The story of Arachne. *Metamorphoses*, Ovid

p. 53, line 15: "The fourth nature is water from stone." *Psychology and Alchemy*, C.G. Jung

p. 53, line 16: "On a base of three (triangle), there rises toward the point of its summit the pyramid, which is born from the relation of four points." *I mistici dell'Occidente*, E. Zolla

p. 54, line 6: The film is *Mon oncle d'Amerique*, A. Resnais

p. 54, line 15: The book is *In Search of the Miraculous, Fragments of an Unknown Teaching*. P. D. Ouspensky

p. 56, line 12: The film is *Kaos*. Taviani brothers

p. 58, line 4: *Joseph and His Brothers*, T. Mann

p. 81, line 6 from bottom: "Poem for Nika," Y. Yevtushenko

p. 99, line 3: *Love Story*, H. Hesse. This well-known fable is published in an edition illustrated with watercolors, and is also published under the title *Pictor's Metamorphosis*.

p. 99, line 8: "I don't have time," he said, and she, the fox, gave him the secret, "whatever is essential is invisible to your eyes." *The Little Prince*, A. de Saint-Exupery

p. 101, line 5 from bottom: "Do you know where my strength comes from? I have never been loved." *No Man's Land*, H.Pinter

p. 106, line 3: "What are you doing, Isabel? I'm doing what everyone else is doing, going home . . . . End your story, it was already over before you started." *Passion*, J–L. Godard

p. 118, line 10: *Taoist Chinese Fable. Choi Yun Shi Ma, The Man from the Gobi Who Lost a Horse*

An old Taoist from the Gobi Desert had one son and many horses. One horse was better than all the others. One day this horse got lost. Everyone came running. "We're so sorry about your lost horse."

"There's nothing I can do about it. If the horse had to get lost, let it be lost." People thought it strange that the old man didn't feel bad. Three months later, the horse returned, bringing along a group of wild horses. Everyone ran to the old man to congratulate him. He said, "There's no reason to be so happy. There's nothing special about this." People found this strange.

A year went by. One day the old man's son fell off one of these horses and broke his leg, but the old man was not sad. He said, "Oh, bad luck. We'll do what we can." They took care of the boy, but he was left with a limp. His father was not disturbed. "What had to happen happened." Friends and relatives thought that he had become too old to understand the disaster that had struck his only son. But the old man said, "Thank goodness my son fell from the horse and limps but is still alive." Then he threw a party and invited everyone. People thought he had become senile.

Another year went by, bringing war with the Siberians. The state recruited all the young men. When the officials came to the village, they did not take the crippled boy. They took all of the other village boys. Because the Siberians were strong in battle, they killed all the village boys. In the end, only the old man had children and grandchildren. At last the villagers understood. Losing isn't always bad.

p. 126, line 1: La Maga (the mother of Rocamadur) is the name of the protagonist in *Hopscotch*, J. Cortazar

p. 126, line 3: Useppe is the little boy protagonist in *History*, E. Morante

p. 152, line 6 from bottom: "I condemn you to live in other forms in the den of the serpent and to return to earth each night to run a hundred times around the cemetery that holds your victim's remains . . . "Stone Eyes" in *Fairie's Emerald Book*.